DEAD

RECKONING

(A Kelsey Hawk Mystery—Book 2)

Kate Bold

Kate Bold

Bestselling author Kate Bold is author of the ALEXA CHASE SUSPENSE THRILLER series, comprising six books (and counting); the ASHLEY HOPE SUSPENSE THRILLER series, comprising six books (and counting); the CAMILLE GRACE FBI SUSPENSE THRILLER series, comprising eight books (and counting); the HARLEY COLE FBI SUSPENSE THRILLER series, comprising eleven books (and counting); the KAYLIE BROOKS PSYCHOLOGICAL SUSPENSE THRILLER series, comprising five books (and counting); the EVE HOPE FBI SUSPENSE THRILLER series, comprising seven books (and counting); the DYLAN FIRST FBI SUSPENSE THRILLER series, comprising five books (and counting); the LAUREN LAMB FBI SUSPENSE THRILLER series, comprising five books (and counting); and the KELSEY HAWK MYSTERY series, comprising five books (and counting).

An avid reader and lifelong fan of the mystery and thriller genres, Kate loves to hear from you, so please feel free to visit www.kateboldauthor.com to learn more and stay in touch.

BOOKS BY KATE BOLD

KELSEY HAWK MYSTERY
DEAD INSIDE (Book #1)
DEAD RECKONING (Book #2)
DEAD TO ME (Book #3)
DEAD SILENCE (Book #4)
DEAD TO DAWN (Book #5)

ALEXA CHASE SUSPENSE THRILLER
THE KILLING GAME (Book #1)
THE KILLING TIDE (Book #2)
THE KILLING HOUR (Book #3)
THE KILLING POINT (Book #4)
THE KILLING FOG (Book #5)
THE KILLING PLACE (Book #6)

ASHLEY HOPE SUSPENSE THRILLER
LET ME GO (Book #1)
LET ME OUT (Book #2)
LET ME LIVE (Book #3)
LET ME BREATHE (Book #4)
LET ME FORGET (Book #5)
LET ME ESCAPE (Book #6)

CAMILLE GRACE FBI SUSPENSE THRILLER
NOT ME (Book #1)
NOT NOW (Book #2)
NOT WELL (Book #3)
NOT HER (Book #4)
NOT NORMAL (Book #5)
NOT AGAIN (Book #6)
NOT SAFE (Book #7)
NOT TODAY (Book #8)

HARLEY COLE FBI SUSPENSE THRILLER
NOWHERE SAFE (Book #1)
NOWHERE LEFT (Book #2)

PROLOGUE

The panting was the worst of it.

No, that was not quite true. The fact that she knew she would die was the worst of it—the panting coming from the monster behind her only made things worse. She ran as fast as her frozen limbs would carry her, cracking against the hard ice that made thunderous sounds below, trying to ignore the icy wind that cut her cheeks like shards of glass. Trying to ignore the snarls of the beast as it closed in on its prey.

She couldn't hide. Her breath, the last few she would breathe in this world, escaped her lips in large bursts of white, rising like a beacon to show it exactly where she was. She had learned about smoke signals in school, and it only came back to mind now. Knowledge that had been lost until her life flashed before her eyes, and it was still useless.

The woman tried to hold her breath, but it was impossible when she was running as fast as she could. If she held it for a few steps, the white tendrils leaped up instantly and abundantly to call out to the pursuer. It would still track her even if she were not breathing so heavily. She had known that when she first looked into its eyes. Her oncoming death was old news—she knew she was dead from the moment she looked into the dark eyes—now, it was toying with her.

But human instinct told her there was a chance. If only she could run faster, move for a minute more, get to the lights in the distance that never seemed to get any closer. If only she could live for a moment more, then she might survive. If she had not been running, she would have laughed. Even as her brain told her to keep going, she knew she was lying to herself.

The frozen lakes often became mirrored at the start of winter before the snow dusted them with a blanket of snow. The rivers did not—the rushing water twisted and snapped into uneven ripples that refracted the light and sucked it in. She did not need a mirror to know there was terror in her eyes.

Another shiver ran through her body, threatening to topple her. Still, the panting came from behind, and she did not dare turn to check how close it was, or she would freeze in place. She had been naive

1

enough to think she had escaped, but he had let her go to torment her more.

Her foot went through the ice and into the water below. Her bare foot numbed—the water was colder than ice. She gasped as it cut through her and ran up her leg toward her heart. She grabbed her thigh, wrenched her leg from the cold, and moved even though she felt unable. She stumbled through the two-inch deep snow, limping and favoring her numb left leg.

Please! Please let the cold kill me!

She wore a thin T-shirt, already wet from the thin mist hanging in the air, and her pants clung to her legs, soaked from the kicked-up water and unfortunate breaks through the ice. She was not running for her life anymore; she was running for her death. She only had to outlast the beast, and the cold would claim her. She clouds slip into the numbness with no more pain. She would not have to look into his eyes again, or recoil from his glistening teeth, or cower from his sheer size and power.

She stopped. The silence was the most terrifying thing she had ever heard. The woman looked wildly around, trying to find the beast. The moon shone down from above, the stars twinkling in the black sky, and the white snow brightened the night. She could see all in every direction, but she could not see it. She covered her mouth and breathed through her nose, hoping to remain concealed even though she did not have a hiding spot.

Bushes stood to her right, a tree line fifty paces to the left. She could feel the water rumbling below the ice, her soles numb, and the tremoring of the rushing water moving up her like an earthquake. She had to make a decision: left or right. She took a shaky breath and focused on the bushes. They were closer—she could hide there.

A deep exhalation of breath sent ice flowing through her veins. She had not been cold out in the vast desolate landscape with scraps of clothing covering her body or when she had plunged her foot into the unforgiving water. She only truly knew what cold was when she felt the chill of its breath on the back of her neck.

Her choice was not the trees or bushes; it was to fight or run. The beast had come for her; death had come for her, but she could prolong her life even if she could not escape death.

Trembling, she took a step forward and away from the beast. Perhaps she could sneak away unnoticed. Then she ran. She only made it two steps before her feet betrayed her, and she fell, spinning and sprawling to the ground. She looked up at the night sky, wishing upon a star, but her wish did not come true.

The face of the beast replaced the beauty of the night, snarling with flashing teeth. It covered the blackness as it pounced on her, smashing her through the ice and into the waiting death below.

The water numbed her instantly—comforted her in its cold embrace. The eyes of the beast looked down into hers as it pushed her down into the depths of hell, and she could only smile. The monster could not terrorize her anymore.

She slipped away into the darkness, finally welcoming death.

CHAPTER ONE

Special Agent Kelsey Hawk twisted the coiled phone cord as she waited to be connected to the ex-detective who might help her find the person who slaughtered her family. She had called multiple times over the past few weeks, and he had not picked up the phone once. She let it ring out before placing the old phone on the receiver. She tapped it a couple of times before opening her laptop.

It was not much, but it was all she had gotten her hands on so far. No one liked a cop looking into old unsolved cases—it was like a kick in the teeth. You didn't solve the case, and I think I can. What it really said was: you are not good at your job. It was especially worse when the cop was a Special Agent in the FBI, and the victims were the agent's family. Kelsey's mother, father, and younger sister were brutally murdered in a home invasion. The case had gone unsolved for twenty years, and Kelsey knew there was little chance of solving it after all this time, but she had to try.

Her career in the FBI had consumed her for years, driven toward her line of work by a thirst for justice. She had looked at the case files before but had not delved into the case. Perhaps she was scared about what she might find—why had she been allowed to live when her entire family had been slain? She'd not had the time to consider the case before, but since being shipped off to a small town in North Dakota, she had all the time in the world.

When not catching serial killers!

She hovered the cursor over the folder on the desktop marked *CS Photos*. She had been putting off looking at them and didn't know if she would. She could still remember how grotesque they had looked when she had lived through it as a child. She was only ten when it happened and had only escaped the killer's clutches by hiding in the closet. Kelsey didn't have the strength to look at the crime scene photos of her dead family.

The window offered a much more appealing view. Her new apartment, slightly bigger than the temporary one she had been housed in when she first moved to Winchburgh, looked over the Balsam River.

Most of the rivers in Vanburgh County converged or merged at points, and she knew this river fed into the river that ran through the City of Bridges. She had almost died there after plunging into the river to stop a killer taking young women to relive his childhood monstrosities. She shivered at the thought.

I would do it all again if it meant keeping someone like him off the streets.

It was home now. When she had moved to Winchburgh, thanks to her Special Agent in Charge back at the FBI office in sunny Valleyview, Kelsey hoped for a speedy expedition. He was still out to get her, meaning she would not leave small-town North Dakota any time soon. Not that she was in any rush anymore. Since working the biggest case in Vanburgh County history and getting to know the locals, she found that the place wasn't so bad. Even if they still had four more months of snow to contend with.

The snow created a clean blanket of white over the entire state, and it would be beautiful if only it were not so cold all of the time. Kelsey had been used to beaches and warmth, and now, she had this. She stared out into the white expanse outside.

No time to daydream when there is work to be done.

With spare time on her hands after solving the previous case, she had vowed to solve her family's case or look into it, and it was slow going. She was still waiting on some of the case files being sent over, but everything was being blocked by red tape and procedure. That was not abnormal, but she couldn't help but think her previous SAC was hindering her progress with his sick and twisted games. She took out her cell phone and brought up the last message from Paul Granger, her ex-Special Agent in Charge.

We all get lucky sometimes. Good thing you didn't get anyone killed with your recklessness. Don't worry, I'm waiting for you to mess this up, as always.

It should have been much simpler in a small town, but her life was more complex and complicated here.

Now that I'm looking into the deaths of my family, I'm sure my life will be anything but simple... or easy.

The worst of it all was having to relive it. For the past two weeks, the nightmares had come. She was back in her childhood home, walking through the halls, her family already dead. She was cursed in her dreams to wander the halls forever, knowing someone was in the house with her. Every room she came across had a dead body in it.

Each time she woke, she was comforted by the white snow outside, a welcome replacement for the red in her dreams.

Kelsey shook her head—she needed to concentrate, or she would get nowhere. She had less to do at work, but there were still plenty of administrative tasks, and she would not have extra time for long.

She opened up some of the files on her laptop, checking for the fifth or sixth time the files she had been sent. The neighbors had been interviewed the morning after to check if they had heard or seen anything, but no one had. The deaths occurred in the middle of the night; the three victims were stabbed to death. There was a list of suspects that had committed crimes in the area during that time, but they all led nowhere. More than half of them were dead, and a handful were now in prison. Kelsey was still waiting on the forensics from the crime scene and any other files from the investigation. She had not directly looked at the case, but she knew there was not much. They had no leads to chase, so there was nowhere to go. Still, she was determined to do something.

Kelsey picked up the phone again and dialed the number she had memorized. She stared out the window absently but was startled from her daydreams by the phone being answered.

"Will you stop calling this number!" Harvey Waters demanded.

"I will when you talk to me," Kelsey replied.

She grabbed her notebook and a pen, hoping to get something down on paper. Something told her she was only going to have one chance to talk with him.

"Listen, I get that you think you are some hotshot in the FBI because you have a decent track record, and I know you like to break the rules, but you are not special, Hawk."

Kelsey wanted to correct him and mention she was a special agent, but she didn't want to lose him. He was disrespecting her, but she let it slide while she had him on the line.

When she had requested more case files, someone had taken notice, and she suspected it was her old SAC. Whoever it was must have spread the word, and Harvey Waters had been expecting her call.

"I don't think I'm special," Kelsey agreed. "My family were slaughtered, and I deserve answers."

"The best detectives in the city worked that case, and there was nothing. I should know; I was one of the leads."

Sounds like someone has an ego.

"I'm not trying to step on anyone's toes, Mr. Waters. I only want to look at the case myself and see what's there. Times change, and technology improves. He might have done this again if he's still out there, and we can cross-reference cases. When you were working on a case, did you consult anyone else in the department? Did you get a second opinion on things, or did you think you knew it all?"

Kelsey knew she was treading a fine line.

"Your dad was a cop. Everyone worked on this case in some way. We didn't miss anything, and we didn't half-ass anything. Take a look all you want, but you won't find any mistakes or anything missed."

"I'm not accusing you of not doing your job," Kelsey said. "I know it feels like I'm stepping on your toes, but I want to work with you, not against you."

There was silence on the other end of the line.

"Will you talk to me about the case?" Kelsey pleaded.

"Everything is in the case files," Harvey replied.

Kelsey let out a sigh of relief. He was willing to have some sort of conversation about it.

"I've seen what's in some of the files, but I want to hear from you. You worked the case. What did you feel about it? Were there any suspects not in the files? Did you have any hunches? Do you know why they were killed? This wasn't a burglary, was it?"

Kelsey still felt detached from the case, as if she were investigating another murdered family.

"No. it wasn't a burglary. To be honest, we did have a list of people we spoke to off the record, but it was weird."

"Weird?" Kelsey asked.

"It was like we were chasing a ghost. Someone got into that house and killed your parents and sister. They knew what they were doing, and they entered with the intent to kill. They would have known you were in the house. They targeted your parents, but I was never able to figure out why."

Kelsey wrote that down in her notebook: *parents had enemies?*

Her dad had been a cop, but not an important enough one to gain an enemy who would have done this. Still, she made a note to check his arrest record. Her mother was a coroner. Kelsey couldn't imagine that would gain her any enemies, but she would look into that, too.

"During that time, you had disciplinary action for mishandling evidence," Kelsey noted.

"I didn't mess up that case if that's what you are insinuating," Harvey replied curtly.

"I'm not insinuating anything," Kelsey clarified. "It's just weird that a month after that, you were awarded a promotion and taken off the case."

"I wasn't taken off the case; I moved to a different department."

"But you didn't work it anymore. You said everyone worked the case, but you didn't once you transferred."

"Okay, I've had enough of this. If you want to accuse me of something, come out and say it, Hawk."

"Have you spoken to SAC Granger?" Kelsey asked. "Is he trying to slow me down?"

"We're done." Harvey hung up the phone before Kelsey could probe anymore.

Kelsey hadn't gotten anything of value, but she felt she was moving forward. She wrote Harvey's name down on her pad. He wouldn't talk to her again, but she was going to look into him. He sounded upset and definitely knew more than he was letting on. Unless he really was frustrated at not being able to solve the case. She would follow up either way.

Kelsey picked up her cell phone as soon as it rang.

"Special Agent Hawk," Deputy Sheriff John Gallant said. "Balsam River, Ettram Bay, as soon as you can. They've found a body."

CHAPTER TWO

The white tent on the snow-covered ice did not blend in with the surrounding area—it stuck out like a sore thumb. That was only because Kelsey knew there was a dead body below it.

Kelsey surveyed the scene before she went down to the tent. The Balsam River wound its way through Winchburgh, with the wide part in the center of town doubling as a skating rink. Volunteers cleared it nightly through the winter, and a large metal fire pit sat on one bank. It was an inviting place where many locals gathered in the cold to skate and roast marshmallows.

The only experience Kelsey had of skating was going to a local rink once in Mikkisula, Missouri, when she was five or six. She had fallen and hurt her knee—it was enough to put her off skating for good. Kelsey had changed a lot since then, and she knew she had to try skating again if she wanted to properly fit in with the community. If she fell this time, she would get straight back up and keep going.

Kelsey trudged through the snow in her new winter boots, and for once, her toes did not feel frozen and about to fall off. She discovered she could adapt to this situation just as she did to most.

Sheriff Anderson was waiting outside the tent with two other officers. He held out his hand for Kelsey to shake.

"Thanks for coming down so quickly," Sheriff Anderson said.

"Of course," Kelsey replied.

The sheriff was a world away from her former SAC back in Valleyview. For one, he let her do her job and respected her when she did. Like Granger, he would pull her up when things were not done right, but Granger hated Kelsey and was out to get her. Sheriff Anderson was more like a father who didn't tolerate any nonsense but wanted the best for everyone around him.

"What do we have so far?" Kelsey asked.

"Young woman with her leg trapped in the ice. She must have frozen to death." The Sheriff sighed. "Don't know much more than that yet. Deputy Gallant is in there right now, taking a look, and forensics are on their way. I really hope we don't have another serial killer on our hands."

"If we do, I will catch him," Kelsey asserted.

Sheriff Anderson looked at her and allowed himself a small smile. "I know you will, Special Agent Hawk. That's why we needed you here. Take a look and tell me what you think."

Kelsey nodded, catching the eyes of the other officers at the scene. She nodded to them, too, reassuring them that everything would be fine. She was used to this sort of thing, coming from a large metropolitan city—the death, not the cause—but it was more peaceful out here. One death rocked the entire town, and they were still coming to terms with the body found at the winter festival, even if it was not a local woman.

Back in Valleyviw, a death like that would have been shocking, but people would still go about their regular lives. Things like this didn't happen in small towns. Even though the previous case had been solved, people were still on edge. If it were a local woman this time, people would be more than just on edge. Deaths like this didn't just affect the people connected, but the entire town. If Kelsey didn't get ahead of this, it would change everything—two killers in the same year would have a devastating effect.

Investigating murders in the city was about catching the killer— investigating a murder in Winchburgh was about preventing hysteria.

Kelsey pushed the flaps aside and entered. Deputy John Gallant was squatted over the body, taking in the scene. He wore lycra gloves, and his fingers must have been freezing. He stood up when he saw Kelsey and reached into his pocket, taking out another pair of gloves and tossing them to her. Kelsey grabbed them in her gloved hands but didn't put them on yet—her fingers were cold enough in the padded gloves.

"It's good to see you," John said.

"Considering the circumstances," Kelsey added.

"You know what I mean." John looked down at the body. "I think she escaped from somewhere."

Kelsey didn't ask yet why he thought that; she wanted to check the body first and look over it with a fresh set of eyes, unbiased by anything anyone else had spotted. It was not difficult to determine why the deputy thought that. Her wrists were red from rubbing against something, and there were no marks typical of cuffs or zip ties. She had been tied up with rope, and she had struggled against the rope for a while—she had eventually escaped and had ended up trapped in the ice.

I don't buy it. She escaped and got herself trapped. It all feels too unfortunate.

Kelsey moved around the body, taking it all in. The woman looked in her mid-twenties, possibly a little younger. She wore a thin t-shirt and pants, both frozen completely—they had been soaked before freezing. The woman's skin was taught and blue, her hair frozen to her head.

"She was in the water at some point," Kelsey said. "She was bound, being held hostage maybe, and she escaped. I want someone to check along the river in both directions for where she went in."

John nodded. "This sort of weather, you measure survival time in minutes, especially with what she was wearing."

One of the woman's lower legs was caught in the ice where her foot had plunged through. She lay on her back, the knee bent on the leg with the stuck foot and the other foot sprawled out to one side. Her arms were out to each side, but the body did not seem posed. She had died while stuck in the ice, and her body had fallen backward.

The woman wore no shoes or no shoe on the visible foot, but Kelsey was confident it would be the same with the other.

"You saw the blisters on the foot?" Kelsey asked.

John nodded again. "She was running from someone or somewhere."

Kelsey leaned down near the foot and studied it. It was pale from the cold, but there were red burst blisters on the soul from running on hard ground, likely ice. She had cut her foot pretty badly, and if blood was left somewhere close, they might be able to trace where she came from.

"Her foot is dirty," Kelsey said.

"Dirty?" John asked, crouching close beside Kelsey.

"She came down the bank somewhere where the snow was thin, and dirt became trapped in the creases. She was running, headed for the river, and went through at some point but managed to get out. Maybe whoever was pursuing her fished her out so they could chase her some more."

"What makes you think that?" John asked.

"The marks on her shoulders."

John quickly got up and moved around to the other side of the body.

"I can't be sure, but it looks like someone held her by the shoulders at some point, and my best guess is that he did it here."

Kelsey couldn't be sure it was a man, but the death fit better with the profile of a male killer. She was already getting into his mindset to catch him better.

"So," Kelsey continued, "he had her tied up somewhere, and she escaped, or he let her go for some reason. She came to the river, fell in, and either got out by herself or he pulled her out. She ran again, and her foot went through the ice. I don't think she got stuck here—he held her in place, and she was too weak to fight. She died with him right beside her."

John sighed, the white cloud escaping and floating to the tent's ceiling. He might be second in command in Winchburgh and had commanded a unit in the army, but this was still new to him, too. John had seen death, but not like this.

"Stay here until forensic get here, and don't let anyone touch the body before then."

"Where are you going?" John asked.

"I need to take a walk."

Kelsey left the tent and held the sheriff's gaze for a moment but didn't say anything. She looked downriver toward the town and then up the river in the opposite direction.

You were running toward the town, trying to get to safety.

Kelsey walked upriver away from the town. She walked for around five minutes before she found the hole in the ice. She didn't get too close in case the ice cracked, but she saw something floating in it. She stood back up and pulled out her phone to call John, but when she looked back toward the tent, she found him almost at her position.

She wanted to scold him like a small child for leaving the body, but she was going to ask him to bring down an evidence bag. She almost laughed when she saw him hold one up.

"I thought you might need backup. I also had a hunch you would be the one to find something," John said. "Besides, the body is not going anywhere, and the sheriff is there. What did you find?"

"Looks like a wallet. I didn't want to get too close."

"Allow me." John planted his feet with each step to check the ice below, and when he was close enough to the large opening, he crouched down and picked up the wallet, dropping it into the evidence bag."

"I don't know how you can walk around in this cold with just those gloves on," Kelsey noted.

"The army teaches you a lot of things. Adapting to extreme temperatures is one of them. I'll put my wool gloves back on soon, but I'm not in danger of frostbite yet."

"This way," Kelsey said, taking them farther from the town. "We're on the right track; we just need to find where she came down the bank."

The two walked silently, trudging through the snow in search of something that could point them in the right direction. The scenery didn't change. The river wound back and forth, everything covered in the same bleak whiteness. Kelsey thought about turning back several times, but instinct drove her forward. The woman had run—she had tried to escape, likely done so while terrified and wore no shoes. Kelsey owed it to her to continue until she found something, and if that meant walking forever in the comfort of warm boots and clothing, she would. The cold did not numb her; the fear the woman must have felt did.

Kelsey spotted the indentations in the snow on the west bank after walking away from the crime scene for at least fifteen minutes. Someone slid down the bank, likely on their feet and rear. The snow had covered any footprints but had not fully filled the indentations. They stopped short of it and went up the bank to avoid disturbing the marks. Kelsey and John worked their way slowly along the bank unit close to where she had gone down to the river. They found ropes not far back from the spot, amongst some bushes.

They didn't bag them just yet, waiting for someone to come and photograph them in place first.

"They were cut," John said.

"Yeah," Kelsey agreed. "Whoever had her captive released her here. They wanted her to think she could escape and then chased her down on the river."

"That's horrific," John said. "Who would do something like this."

"We will find out," Kelsey assured.

John dipped into the evidence bag as they waited for someone to document the evidence and then drive them back to the tent. He opened the frozen wallet carefully, and his face dropped.

"Crap!"

"What is it?" Kelsey asked.

"I know her," John said. "Becky Samson."

"Is she from the town?" Kelsey asked.

"Yeah, born and raised here. She left to go to university but returns for all the major holidays and when school is out." He let out a long sigh. "Becky and Sheriff Anderson's daughter went to junior high together—they were pretty close for a while. Becky was the star athlete at her high school; I don't know if she kept that up at university."

"Sheriff Anderson can't be the one to talk with the family first. You and I should do it. He's too close to it," Kelsey said.

"Agreed. As soon as someone gets here, I'll talk to the sheriff, and then we can go and talk with the family."

"This needs to be handled properly—it's about more than just the Sheriff," Kelsey said. "He knew Becky Samson, but so will most of the town. And if they didn't already, they soon will. People will react to this; if a local woman can be killed, then anyone can. We are not past the previous killing; people grieved the woman found in the ice, and she wasn't a local. I know you have been talking to people, helping them through the previous killing, but this one will be much worse."

CHAPTER THREE

Kelsey let John take the lead—she was getting to know the people and their quirks, but he still knew them far better than she.

"I am so sorry for your loss," John said. He held Becky's mother's hand in his. "We will need you to come down and identify the body, but we found her wallet close by."

"You're sure it was her?" Mrs. Samson wept.

"I am." John sighed. "I didn't recognize her at first, but it clicked when I found the wallet. Again, I truly am sorry. I know how much Becky meant to this town. Sheriff Andreson will visit you later. He is distraught that something like this happened to Becky. We only ask that you keep it to yourselves for now. Sheriff Anderson wants to speak to his daughter first; she is on a camping trip. He is on his way out there now to pick her up. Once he has spoken to her, and you have had a chance to identify the body formally, he will release a full statement."

"It can't be her," Mrs. Samson sobbed. "She wasn't back in town. It must be someone else, John."

John pursed his lips and patted Mrs. Samson's hand. "I know this is hard, but we will get the son-of-a-bitch who did this. You have my word on that. And if there is anything you need, you only have to ask. We are all here for you."

Mrs.. Samson burst into tears again.

Kelsey was sure it was Becky, too. There were dozens of family photos on the wall, both in the hallway leading from the front door to the living room and in the living room. Pictures showed her growing up from a baby to a young woman. She was with family in some, and others showed her track achievements, documenting her races and taking the podium.

Kelsey could sympathize somewhat with the family. She had lost people she loved, just as the Samsons had. She wanted to console them, but Deputy Gallant was doing that, and she had a job to do. Her instincts told her to keep an eye on the father. He had not shed a tear yet, displaying anger, which was typical in this situation. What was not

15

typical was how he wrung his hands together and fidgeted when he thought no one was looking. He was nervous about something.

"We will get you all the help you need, Mrs. Samson. You don't have to go through this alone," John said.

"I tried to give her the best life," Mrs. Samson murmured. "I didn't grow up with a family, and when I had children, I wanted them to have the best life possible. My parents died not long after I was born. I gave everything to my children, and something like this happens. Who would want to do this to my little girl?"

"We are going to do all we can to find out," John assured. He let go of Mrs. Samson's hand and stood back up from his kneeling position by her chair. He looked around the room before sitting down beside Kelsey on the couch. "This is going to be hard, but we need to ask you a few questions so we can piece together where she might have been leading up to this and who she would have been with."

"We'll help in any way we can," Mr. Samson said efficiently.

Kelsey continued to keep an eye on the father. "You mentioned you have children. Your son, does he live at home?"

"He doesn't. He has an apartment in town with some friends. He's going to be heartbroken when he hears about this. Simon was always the protective older brother."

"We will need to speak to him too, but please refrain from speaking to him about this until we have. As soon as we are done here, we will talk to Simon."

"He wouldn't have done this," Mrs. Samson said, shocked.

"We are not claiming he would, Mrs. Samson. "We need to inform him about Becky's death before he hears it from someone else."

Mrs. Samson nodded.

Kelsey looked at her notebook. "Mrs. Samson, you mentioned that Becky was not supposed to be back in town. Where was she supposed to be?"

"She was attending university in Montana. Becky was studying to be a veterinarian."

"When was she next due back?" Kelsey asked.

"Not for another couple of weeks."

"Could she have come back early?" John asked. "I remember one time she surprised you with a visit."

"She might have," Mrs. Samson admitted. "I don't know." She covered her face with her handkerchief and blew her nose.

16

"When was the last time you spoke to her?" John asked. "You and Becky were close, weren't you?"

"We were," Mrs. Samson admitted. "I spoke to her on the phone… maybe a week ago? Six days? She usually calls more, but I figured she was busy with schoolwork."

"She has a boyfriend in Montana?" Kelsey asked the father while Mrs. Samson was blowing her nose.

He stopped fidgeting when he was being addressed and shrugged his answer with a shake of the head: no.

"She didn't," Mrs. Samson confirmed when she had recovered. "She would have told me if she did."

"Could she have one secretly and not want to tell anyone?" Kelsey probed.

Mrs. Samson shook her head.

"Of course, she could have," Mr. Samson said. "It's not like we knew everything about her. She might have been seeing someone out there and not told us, but chances are she wasn't."

"She did tell us about a couple of guys she was interested in," Mrs. Samson added.

"That never went anywhere," Mr. Samson said. "She was more interested in her studies. Becky is a bright girl, and everyone loves her. She could have boyfriends if she wanted, but she put her studies first. She dreamed of being a veterinarian ever since she was five years old. She won't get to do that, will she?"

Kelsey stared at Mr. Samson, hoping to discover something more than anger, but there was only the burning rage of a father who had lost his daughter. She pitied them and was jealous of them. They had lost their daughter, but they had the community's support. Kelsey had been left alone at the age of ten. That was twenty years ago. There was every chance she would find Becky's killer, but she had little hope of finding her family's killer.

"We know who she ran around with in town, but if you have a list of people she knew in Montana, that would be helpful," John said softly.

Mrs. Samson nodded.

Kelsey was glad John was here with her. She tried to be compassionate, but being compassionate was different when you knew the people and lived in the same community. The community had accepted her for bringing a serial killer to justice, but she was still an outsider and had not completely settled in yet.

17

Maybe that was for the best. She would talk to John after, but she felt there was something lost when you got too close to people. Did John see how the father acted objectively, or was he so close that he only saw a father in grief?

"How did he kill her?" the father asked suddenly.

"He?" Kelsey replied.

"Someone kills a young woman. It's a good bet that it's a man, right?" Mr. Samson asked as if looking for more information.

"We don't know anything yet," John replied. "We'll keep you updated with anything we do discover."

They had decided not to tell the parents about the ropes found on the bank or how Becky might have died, except for informing them she had frozen in the river and it was being treated as suspicious. Their child was gone, and that was enough heartbreak for now.

"One final question before we go," Kelsey said, looking at the father again. "Is there anyone you know of who might want to hurt your daughter?"

Mr. Samson didn't answer, but his wife did. "No, no one would want to harm her. Everyone loves her, and she is friends with everyone in town. It was the same in Montana."

"From what she told us," Mr. Samson added.

"If you think of anything else, please call me," John said, standing. "We'll go to Simon's apartment and notify him of the news. Sheriff Anderson will visit later and inform you of the next steps. I recommend staying put until then. Can you do that?"

Mrs. Samson nodded.

"I'll show you out," Mr. Samson said, staring at Kelsey.

The three walked to the door, and Kelsey scanned the main hallway again. So many photos of Becky at track and cross-country meets—she ran short and long distances.

Is that part of it? Did the killer want to make her run?

"Thank you, John," Mr. Samson said when they arrived at the door. He held out his hand, and John shook it. He did the same for Kelsey. "Thank you, too." When he took her hand, he held it. "I didn't want to say this in front of my wife," he whispered. "Can we go outside for a moment?"

Kelsey nodded. They went outside, and Mr. Samson pulled the door behind him so it was not fully closed but gave a buffer so his wife would not hear.

"Our son is a troubled young man. I know this will come out, so you might as well hear it from me, but I don't want you to think I'm accusing him of anything, but we threw him out of the house six months ago."

John frowned. "What happened?"

"Things were found on his laptop." Mr. Samson sighed. "Disturbing things. I don't know where he got them, and I don't care. He tried to claim his laptop was hacked, but I'm not that stupid." He leaned in a little closer. "This was not normal stuff. Pictures of women tied up; some sexual, and some not. Some stuff about men being superior and having the right to control women. It was hard to see, and it was only the tip of the iceberg. I didn't have to see much before I tossed him out."

"And your wife knows about this?" Kelsey asked.

"It's been a point of contention. She loves her children, and she will do everything for them, and it's one of the many reasons I love her. I know deep down in her core she knows something is wrong with Simon, but she believed what he said. I don't think she wanted to admit that her own child could have stuff like that on his computer. Still, she agreed to ask him to leave the house. He's old enough anyway and needed a kick in the but."

"We will go straight to his home now," John said.

"Check Cooper Bridge," Mr. Samson suggested. "He won't get a regular job no matter how much I try to push him. He got in with a group of guys, and they dealt drugs from under the bridge. They like to hang out there too. I would try there first before you go to his apartment, and if you want to arrest him for dealing, that's alright with me. He needs a bigger kick in the ass than I can give him."

Kelsey pursed her lips and nodded slightly. She felt more pity for the family—they had already lost their son, and now their daughter was dead.

"Mr. Samson, one last thing before we go," Kelsey said. "You mentioned that your son had some derogatory stuff on his laptop about women, but what makes you think he would go after his sister?"

"I don't think he would do that. No matter what he's into, he's always loved his sister. It's just… she was the one who found the stuff on his laptop and brought it to me. When he found out, he went crazy and threatened everyone, including my wife. It tore her apart to see him like that. Becky had it the worst. He called her every name under the sun." Mr. Samson rubbed his head as he struggled to get the words out.

"The last time they saw each other, Simon told Becky that he wished she were dead."

CHAPTER FOUR

John pulled his black truck up to the curb a short distance from the bridge. Numerous youths and adults were congregated, some of them huddled around homemade fires in metal containers like homeless people. This was a side of Winchburgh that Kelsey had not seen yet.

The town was tight-knit, and everyone knew everyone—that meant there was not a lot of crime. Of course, that meant there was still some crime, and Kelsey guessed that most of it occurred under or around Cooper Bridge, which sat in the middle of what could be called an industrial area.

Kelsey didn't like it. It felt like they were walking into the lion's den and straight into trouble.

"What do you know about Simon Samson?" Kelsey asked as they looked toward the bridge.

"If he is dealing drugs, he's flown under the radar so far. This bridge is well known to the department, and we come down here occasionally to shake it down, but it's mostly marijuana and other soft drugs. Sometimes, illegal booze and cigarettes. The bikers run most of the town, but they let these kids down here do their thing because they are small-time."

"How do you want to play this?" Kelsey wanted insight from the man who knew everything about Winchburgh.

"To be honest, I don't know Simon all that well. Most of the folk down here are harmless, but it might be best if you take the lead. You are FBI, which might scare them enough to comply fully."

"I like the sound of that," Kelsey replied, happy to take the lead.

"Let me just scope out the lay of the land before we fully infiltrate the bridge," John said.

Kelsey smiled. He was not a soldier anymore, but he sure acted like one at times. That had its benefits. They both exited the vehicle and walked down toward the bridge. As they got closer, people began to get nervous; bottles were held behind their backs, and some people tossed things into the fires.

"We're not here to cause any trouble," Kelsey said. "We just want to talk to someone."

There were murmurs from the gathered people, around two dozen of them. Kelsey looked at John, who was still surveying the area.

He looked back into the crowd and boomed, "Where is Simon Samson?"

There was no immediate answer, but eventually, someone raised a hand and pointed toward the area under the bridge.

"Thank you," John said.

They walked through the crowd, and Kelsey scanned everyone. She was on edge, ready to give chase at the drop of a hat. She wasn't expecting him to run—they were only here to talk to him about his sister—but it was an enclosed space, and people were already spooked. She tried to keep a neutral expression on her face.

We really are not here to cause any trouble.

Kelsey caught sight of him even though she had not seen a picture. She relied on John to identify him—he knew almost everyone in town. Kelsey only knew it was him by how he nervously looked back at her. He stood with another young man, both of them around twenty-two, and they were talking heatedly. Simon tried to pass something to the other man, but he wouldn't take it. Kelsey nudged John and indicated with a nod of the head where Simon was. John looked at him and nodded, too—that was their man.

"Simon Samson!" John called out. "We just want a word with you."

Simon looked at them but didn't answer back. He hissed at the man he was talking to and received some strong language in return.

Don't you dare run, Simon!

She had no sooner thought it than he did. Simon took the man he was arguing with by the collar and tossed him to the ground before he sprinted off. The man was on his feet instantly and took off running in the same direction.

Kelsey and John ran together as quickly as they could, pushing through the thin crowd.

Where are you going, Simon?

If he had killed her, why had he stuck around? It didn't make sense to Kelsey, but people who did things like that often didn't think like others did. Maybe he thought he could get away with it. That only made Kelsey more determined, and she matched John for speed as they rounded the bridge support and descended the river bank after the two men, one identified and the other not.

They were halfway down when Simon turned and brandished his gun.

"Gun!" John shouted, diving onto Kelsey.

She looked up to see the unidentified man dive to the ground, too. Simon waved the gun, but she could see, even from this distance, that he had no intention of shooting them. Kelsey couldn't lie there and do nothing. She wriggled out from under John and ran toward the river, where Simon was jumping onto a snowmobile. He turned a key and revved the handle, peeling away from the bank with the gun still in his hand.

Kelsey saw her chance. The two had driven here on the snowmobiles, and both were making their escape the same way. Kelsey was not going to let him escape her. She ran as fast as she could through the deep snow as the second man jumped onto the second snowmobile.

Kelsey dived through the air, slamming into the man as he was reaching for the keys. They rolled off together into the snow. John grabbed the back of the man's collar, wrenching him up from the ground, and he pulled her away from Kelsey.

"See what he knows," she said. "I'm going after Simon."

"He's got a gun," John warned.

"So do I," Kelsey said.

She didn't wait for John to try to talk her out of it. She turned the key in the snowmobile, and it rumbled to life. As Simon had done, she turned the throttle on the handlebars, and the vehicle shot forward. She realized she had no idea how to drive a snowmobile when she was in motion.

Kelsey learned quickly. When she turned the throttle more, the snowmobile went faster. When she moved the handlebars, she went left or right. She only had to work out where the brake was, but she could figure that out later. All that mattered was catching Simon. He would be arrested for threatening a police officer and for whatever he was trying to pass off to his friend. There might also be the additional charge of murdering his sister.

The Balsam River wound through the town, so Kelsey didn't have sight of Simon, but he had left her a trail. She followed the snowmobile track that was freshly laid above the frozen river. The adrenaline pumped through her, and she was not scared, but there was a thought in the back of her mind that she might go through the ice. Becky had fallen through the ice and must have only weighed a little over a hundred pounds.

Kelsey had gone through the ice once before when chasing a serial killer and had no intention of doing it again. The chill from the freezing water still lurked within her.

Kelsey turned another bend onto a long, straight portion of the river and saw him a hundred yards ahead. She turned the handle, slowly rotating it almost as far as it would go until the snowmobile neared top speed. She had to catch him, not only because he might be a murderer, but because of what was coming up. They were headed straight toward the middle of town, and even though it was a school day and the middle of the afternoon, there would still be people skating on the wide part of the river.

The revving engine drowned out everything else. They left the industrial part of town and moved into the residential area. She glanced down quickly at the speedometer and saw she was going fifty miles an hour. It felt a lot faster, but still a speed that could do serious harm if they crashed. Kelsey didn't care. She tugged on the throttle more, pushing the vehicle faster.

When she pulled up alongside Simon, he almost got the fright of his life.

"Pull over!" Kelsey shouted.

Simon looked down at the gun and then at Kelsey. Kelsey replied by carefully pulling aside her jacket to show her gun. Some of the wind was knocked from him when he saw it.

"I've spent hours at the shooting range. How's your shot at this speed, Simon!" Kelsey shouted, raising her voice so he could hear her over the droning of the engines.

He decided not to use the gun—he used the snowmobile as a weapon instead. He turned the handlebars sharply and slammed his snowmobile into hers. Kelsey barely kept control of her vehicle, but she managed to keep it going in a straight line. She rounded the bend after him, pushing the vehicle until it was beside his again.

Simon was frustrated and turned the handlebars again. Kelsey was ready for him this time. She had not yet located the brakes, but she let go of the throttle a little, and it was enough for her to fall behind so she was not hit. As soon as she was, she pushed it again to speed up. Simon had to wrench the handlebars in the other direction to compensate. He wove from side to side, almost hitting the rocks on the left.

The skating rink was in the distance, and at least half a dozen people were on it. The zig-zagging of Simon's snowmobile had slowed him, and Kelsey saw her chance. Instead of pulling up fully beside him, she slammed the front of her snowmobile into the back end of his, causing him to fishtail again. He couldn't control it a second time, and he spun in a full circle, almost coming to a stop.

He pulled on the throttle as soon as he was facing the right direction and took off toward the skating rink ahead. Kelsey pulled up beside him and didn't give him any more warnings. The ice rink was only thirty yards in front, and she couldn't risk him going any faster toward the people.

Kelsey stood up on her snowmobile and leaped onto Simon, knocking him off his seat. They rolled on the ground together and came to a stop with a thump. Kelsey quickly rose to her feet to track the snowmobiles, watching them slam harmlessly into the large pile of snow cleared over the weeks from the rink. Screams rang out from the ice rink, but no one was injured.

She turned back to Simon when she heard him groan. It all happened in slow motion. When she faced him, he was lying on his back in the snow and raised the gun in both hands toward her. She knew instinctively he would not fire the gun and would only use it to try and get away, but she had no time for that. As she turned, and in one swift motion, she kicked the gun from his hands. Kelsey spun around fully to face Simon again, his eyes wide in surprise. He screamed in pain, shaking his hand, his fingers hanging limply.

The gun fell into the snow and was still visible.

Simone moved to get up from where he lay, but Kelsey pulled her gun.

"Simon Samson, you are under arrest. You have the right to remain silent. Anything you do say can and will be used against you in court. You have the right to a lawyer. If you cannot afford a lawyer, one will be appointed. If you decide to answer questions now without a lawyer present, you have the right to stop answering at any time."

Kelsey kept the gun on Simon and grabbed his arm, lifting him to his feet.

"You make the slightest move, and I won't hesitate to take you down," Kelsey said. "Do you understand me?"

Simon nodded. He didn't like this one bit, but he knew better than to fight back.

Let's find out why you were so eager to get away from me.

25

CHAPTER FIVE

Kelsey sat in the passenger seat of the cop car that had come to drive Simon back to the station. She didn't react as he fired insults at them, gaining his confidence back by the time they got to the police station. Kelsey instructed the officer driving not to say a word.

John drove behind them in his truck while the non-identified suspect was taken in a separate police car so he would not have a chance to talk with Simon.

As soon as they entered the station, some of his confidence was drained by the energy in the room. Word had gotten around to most of the cops in town that Becky Samson was dead and that Simon had tried to make a run for it, but that was not public knowledge yet. They all watched him as he was escorted into the station. The glares from the cops sucked some of the life from Simon, and he became visibly worried.

"Officer James, I want Mr. Samson thoroughly searched and placed in an interrogation room. I want to talk to him before anyone else does."

"Yes, ma'am," Officer James replied. He took Simon by the shoulder and led him away.

Kelsey sighed in relief and rolled her shoulder to stretch the muscle. She had landed awkwardly, and it ached a little. Nothing a good sleep and a little time wouldn't fix.

"Fred Applegate," Deputy Gallant said as he entered the reception area. "That's the other guy. He's known to a couple of the officers here, but only for petty crimes. He comes from a known family in the community too."

"Did he say anything on the way in?" Kelsey asked.

"Nothing of use, but we can question him after we talk to Simon. He was worried, though. My best guess would be they had drugs on them, but more than usual or stronger stuff. He wouldn't say much in the car, but we get him in a room with a lawyer, and I'm sure he will speak."

26

"If we find the stuff," Kelsey noted. "The river was too winding to keep track of Simon. They didn't drop the stuff at the bridge, so Simon must have taken it. I sent a couple of volunteers to walk the river between the rink and the bridge to see if he tossed it from the snowmobile."

"That was some crazy stuff, by the way. Are you going to take down a bunch of terrorists in a high-rise office building yet? Did you really jump from your snowmobile to his?"

"All in a day's work." Kelsey smiled. "Besides, we weren't going all that fast."

"And that makes it better?" Chief Anderson asked from behind.

Kelsey almost jumped in fright. "You're back," she managed.

"I'm heading over to see the Samsons right now. My daughter is at home and not taking it well at all. Listen, Hawk, we've just lost one community member and don't need to lose another. He had a gun. Even if you were sure he wouldn't shoot you, we all know what can happen accidentally. You could have been killed. Simon Samson could have been killed. I'm glad I don't have to go over there and explain why their son has also died. Although, I have to go and explain why he's been arrested. I've instructed everyone. We don't mention Simon Samson is a suspect until you've thoroughly questioned him, okay?"

"Understood," Kelsey replied.

Sheriff Anderson looked between Kelsey and John before he walked toward the door. He stopped short and turned around. "Hawk! Good job out there. If you hadn't stopped him, he would have plowed straight through the rink, and someone might have got hurt."

Kelsey nodded. She felt an overwhelming sense of pride whenever the sheriff complimented her work, something severely lacking when she was back in the Valleyview office.

"I guess you are the favorite now," John joked when the sheriff had left the building.

"Special Agent Hawk," Officer James said, arriving back, "I found nothing on him. He's in interrogation room two."

"Thank you, officer," Kelsey replied.

He nodded at her. From the looks she got, they felt the same when she gave them plaudits as she felt when she got them from the sheriff. People had regarded her warily when she had first arrived in town, but she had gained their respect by stopping Richard Gibson from claiming more victims.

"You want to do this together?" John asked.

"Let's do it," Kelsey replied.

They walked through the police station together until they got to interview room two. Kelsey looked through the small glass window to see Simon Samson handcuffed to the table. He was sat back in the chair, his wrists leaning on the metal table in front. He was sitting at an angle with one leg up on the corner of the table. If he were not handcuffed to the table, he would look like a man who did not have a care in the world.

John entered first, followed by Kelsey. Simon showed no sign that he heard them—he noticed them more when John walked straight to the corner of the table and forcefully pushed Simon's leg from it.

"Show some respect," John demanded.

"I could say the same," Simon replied.

John stood behind Simon and looked like he would slap him on the head.

Kelsey sat down on the opposite side of the table. "Do you have any idea how much trouble you are in, Simon?"

"Enlighten me," Simon said, sneering at Kelsey.

He had regained all of his confidence, and the subject matter on his computer affected him. Simon had no respect for authority, but it was obvious that he hated women. Kelsey had seen the venom in his eyes when she knocked him from the snowmobile and disarmed him. He had been scared and hated that he was scared of a woman. He had the same venom in his eyes now. She needed to disarm him differently.

"How are you feeling after your tumble?" she asked.

That rocked him a little, but he smiled at her. "I've had worse."

"Do you even know how to use a gun?" she asked. "I can teach you if you like."

"You should be grateful I didn't shoot you back on the river," Simon spat.

"Yeah? Is that what you think, Simon? Should women be grateful to you for not killing them? I guess that means most of us should be grateful, but not all of us, right?"

Kelsey wanted to say a lot more, but she held back. She had to do this right so they could get to the bottom of the killing as quickly as possible.

"You're crazy," Simon replied. "You think you can play mind games with me? You're not smart enough."

"Well, Simon. I'm a special agent with the FBI, and you are a petty criminal who deals drugs under a bridge. Only one of us is currently handcuffed to the table. So, please tell me which of us is the smart one."

Simon suddenly lunged from his seat, the handcuffs snapping him back. He smiled wildly, spit dripping from his bottom lips. He breathed heavily, glaring straight at Kelsey.

Kelsey didn't flinch. She turned a page in her notebook and faked a yawn. "So, Simon, what did you toss from your snowmobile? I saw you throw it, but I was too busy to stop."

She had not seen him toss anything, but she hoped he might believe she did.

Simon breathed heavily, annoyed he didn't get the reaction he expected. His face started to turn pink.

"Sit down," John ordered, taking him by the shoulder and pushing him back into his seat. John sat down, too. "Are you done with this? I know your parents, Simon. They are worried about you, so knock off this manly bullshit. Special Agent Hawk chased you down, caught you, knocked you off your snowmobile, disarmed you, and arrested you. Do with that what you will. Now, do I need to go get you a juice box, or will you be a man and face up to what you have done?"

Simon looked at the table and wrung his handcuffed hands together like his father had earlier that day. When he looked up, he wouldn't look Kelsey in the eye.

"I didn't hear you calling after me, Alright? And the gun I have is for hunting."

"The handgun?" John asked. "Come on, you watch all this stuff about men being superior, and you think we would buy that? No one goes hunting with a handgun, Simon."

"Depends on the prey," Simon smiled.

"What have you been hunting, Simon?" Kelsey asked.

"Wouldn't you like to know?" He smiled but still didn't look at her.

Kelsey leaned forward, showing she wasn't afraid of him. He was deranged and needed help, but below it all, he was a desperate young man looking for his place in the world.

Is that enough to become a killer?

"I would very much like to know what you have been hunting, Simon. Deer? Birds? Women?"

Simon finally looked at Kelsey. "Special Agent Hawk, if I didn't know any better, I would think you were hitting on me."

John slammed his fist down on the table, and it startled Simon.

29

"Enough messing around, Simon. We can charge you with brandishing a weapon, threatening a cop, selling illegal substances, resetting arrest, and a dozen other crimes. We won't need to when we charge you with murder."

Kelsey was done with the slow progression and wanted to get to the point, to knock him off balance now that he was in the flow of answering their questions.

"Murder?" Simon said, confused.

"Where were you last night, Simon," Kelsey asked calmly. She was doing her best to talk to him with civility.

"Murder," Simon muttered. He suddenly looked uncomfortable and unsure of himself.

"Becky is dead," Kelsey said. "We found her on the river this morning."

"Becky? What? No, she's in Montana." Simon's face paled, and he looked like he would throw up.

"She found the stuff on your laptop, Simon," John shouted. "She told your parents all about your dark little secrets. You were thrown out of your family home. You turned to a life of petty crime, with the lowest of the low in the town. Your mom supported you, but you know deep down she doesn't believe your lies. They've pretty much disowned you, haven't they?"

"Stop," Simon muttered.

"She's the golden child, and you hated her for that already, but then this! She gets to go off to university while you have to scrape by, hanging out under a bridge. It's no wonder you turned to a life of crime," John continued.

Simon put his head in his bound hands and shook it.

"You hated her, Simon," Kelsey continued. "Not just hate, there was a rage inside you. You wished you could swap places with her, didn't you? You wanted her dead, Simon! You said that, didn't you? You wished Becky was dead!"

"Yeah!" Simon snapped. "Yeah, I did! Is that what you want to hear? She shouldn't have done what she did. Becky needed to know her place. She was a bitch, and I was going to deal with her."

"What did you do to her, Simon? Where did you keep her?" Kelsey asked.

Simon looked back up and shook his head.

"Did she tell you she was returning, or did you lure her here?" John demanded.

30

"I have an alibi," he hissed. "I have an alibi for last night. I didn't kill her."

"Where were you last night, Simon?" John asked.

"I'm not saying anymore until I have a lawyer," Simon said.

Kelsey looked him in the eye. There was too much hatred to discern if he was telling the truth.

"Get a lawyer here as quickly as possible, and then we take his statement. I want to establish if he has an actual alibi, and I want to know today."

CHAPTER SIX

The International Peace Gardens were beautiful at all times of the year, but especially in the winter. The man stood near the fountain at one end of the garden and looked out as far as he could see. The gardens would go through numerous color changes through the seasons, but only in the winter did the color remain the same. Everything was covered in white—it was a permanence he appreciated. The world was going through far too much change, and he liked to have some consistency.

Red, blue, yellow, green, purple, orange, and violet; all the colors of the rainbow mixed in spring and summer to create rows and curves of flowers and trees. When all the colors of light were mixed, they created white light. The snow mimicked that, replacing all the colors with white. He breathed in, taking in the clean, crisp scent of the cold instead of the floral scent that hovered the rest of the year.

It helped him to clear his head and think properly—to look toward the future instead of dwelling on the past.

"Oh, my dear. You will catch a cold!"

The man whipped around, suddenly on guard. He let his guard drop a little when he saw a little old woman standing behind him; she reminded him of someone he used to know, and he tried to control his breathing as he stood before her. She looked him up and down and repeated her claim.

"You will catch a cold, my dear."

He wouldn't, but he didn't need to argue the point. He had gone out in a simple pair of pants and wore no socks under his shoes. The thin sweater he wore on his torso was the only layer on his upper body, and while he wore a thin beanie, it didn't cover his ears. He knew they would be red raw by the time he got home, just like his nose and fingers. He could bear the cold better than most, an immunity he had built up from childhood.

"Come on, I have some extra hot chocolate in my flask," she said.

The old woman took his arm and led him from the fountain to a small pagoda with a bench beneath. She was bundled up in multiple layers, doubling her frail size. He allowed himself to be led to the bench and sat down when she pushed on his arm. It made a welcome change from those who took one look at him and gave him a wide berth. It wasn't always how he dressed—they could see it in his eyes. He was a man who did not fit in society and had once been a boy who did not fit into the world.

"You are going to freeze to death out here," the old woman said.

"No, I won't," he replied with a smile.

The old woman acted as if she had not heard him. She sat down beside him and placed her handbag on her lap. She pulled out a small flask and popped off the lid, which doubled as a cup. She unscrewed the cap, poured some thin hot chocolate into the cup, and handed it to him.

"I always make too much," the old woman noted. "My husband keeps telling me I'm going to die by chocolate because I have too much."

The man smiled back at her, holding the warm cup in his hands. He felt a little of the pain that would come later—it was not the cold that hurt; the cold numbed everything—it was only when the warmth came that the pain appeared. He could feel it in his fingers as the warm cup started to defrost his fingers. He relished the feeling.

"Go on, drink up," the old woman ordered.

The man would normally not be told what to do, but she was being so nice to him that he was compelled to sample some. He did not want to drink too much, or he would become too warm, but he had some. It was thin but sweet—the hot chocolate was made with milk and too much sugar. It was old people's hot chocolate. Once he had taken a few sips, the old woman took the cup back and drank some herself.

The hot chocolate brought some of the pain back as it cascaded down his throat and into his stomach. It burned a hole in him, pain he was saving for later.

"Go on, take some more," she urged, handing the cup back to him.

The man did not want to drink more and bring on more pain just yet, so he pretended to consume more of the hot liquid before handing it back to the old woman.

"What are you doing out here without proper winter clothes?" the old woman asked.

"I don't mind the cold," he replied.

"But you must be freezing," the old woman replied, taking another drink as if just talking about the cold made her colder.

33

"No," the man said. "I don't feel it after a while. Sometimes, I walk in the snow without my shoes on."

"Oh, I can't imagine," the old woman said. "I suppose it is one of those new methods to keep you feeling younger or something like that."

"Something like that," the man agreed.

He looked out at the blanketed peace garden from the bench. A dozen or so people were walking around dressed like the old woman. They didn't appreciate the cold either. They were happy walking around without a care in the world. He despised them, but not as much as he despised the chosen ones—those who had grown up to be happy.

"They don't deserve their happiness," the man muttered.

"Who, my dear? Oh, everyone deserves some happiness," the old woman said.

When the man looked at her, she was smiling at him as if she could solve all of his problems. She reached out and patted his arm with a gloved hand.

She wouldn't touch me with her bare hand, and not because of the cold. She thinks she can save me only because she thinks I need to be saved.

"You look down on me, don't you?" the man asked.

"I'm sorry," the old woman replied.

"I can see it in your eyes. Don't lie to me."

The old woman's eyes widened. "I don't understand what you are saying, young man." She shook her head, flabbergasted to be accused of such a thing.

"Sure, you do," he hissed. "You saw me and knew I needed help, but let me tell you a little secret." The man leaned in to whisper in the old woman's ear. "They tried to help me, but they couldn't. I know exactly what you want to do. You want to mold me into something I am not, and you hide behind your veiled kindness."

"I, um, I don't know what you are talking about. I only wanted to help you."

"I don't need any help," the man snapped. "You don't want to help me; you only want to feel better about yourself. You want to return to your idiotic friends and tell them about the man you saved from the cold. You want them to congratulate you for being such a good person, but it is hollow. It is always hollow."

The old woman quickly screwed the cap on the flask, dumping the rest of the cup on the snow beside the bench. That angered the man the most. The snow was pure, clean, cold—she had ruined it. He thought

34

about smacking her across the face, but he would never get his work done if he did that to everyone who deserved it.

The old woman stood up and really looked down on him this time. The man stared straight ahead at the peace garden, not giving her the pleasure of a dirty look. Much more appealing than going back to her friends and telling them how she had helped someone would be telling them how crazy the person was. She could tell them that if he snarled at her or looked at her a certain way. She might feel bad about how she had treated him if he remained impassive.

The man didn't watch her go, but he listened to the gentle crunch of her footsteps as she hurried away. Old people could move extremely fast when they wanted to. When he could not hear her footsteps anymore, the man tried to ground himself. He needed to rid his body of the warmth the hot chocolate had brought and the reek she had left on him.

He moved feared from the bench into a crouching position and stuck his hands into the snow covering the flower bed before him. He left them there until they were numb. When he pulled his fingers out, they were pale with a tinge of blue. He felt back to his old self. The anger and resentment were gone when he sat back on the bench.

The man reached into his pants pocket and pulled out the small piece of folded paper, the only thing he carried. His fingers were numb, and he fumbled to unfold the paper, and that washed away the last of his irritation. He was not happy; there was never any happiness, but there was contentment. He should wait, just as he had waited between the first two, but he needed more contentment than he currently had, so he had to act.

He looked down the list of names. He did not have a method for the order he would go through them, only that he would go through every single one and ensure order was restored to the world. He looked at each name and waited for one to call out to him. He would take his next victim sooner than expected, but he still did not need to rush it. He looked out over the pace gardens again, soaking in the cold.

The man pitied those dressed in layers to ward off the cold. If they wanted to stay warm, they should have stayed home. They could not truly appreciate the outdoors without experiencing all of it. If he had any inclination to help the general population, he would show them what they were missing. Perhaps after he was done with his list, he could help others find their path in life.

He looked back down on his list and scanned each of the names. He smiled when he saw it. The name shone on the paper as if chosen by divine intervention—he had not noticed it until that day, even though he had been to the gardens on multiple occasions. He ran his finger over the name, nodding to himself before he put the piece of paper away.

The next person had been chosen.

CHAPTER SEVEN

Kelsey looked up from her desk when the sheriff entered. With a new apartment came a new office. The initially assigned FBI special agent to Winchburgh was permanently in Bismarck, and since the personnel had been changed, Kelsey and the sheriff had agreed that the FBI offices needed to be closer to the police station. When the building one block from the station had become unoccupied, they had moved everything from the old FBI office to a new one. It made it easier to liaise with local law enforcement.

"Where are we at, Hawk?" the sheriff asked.

"So far? Nowhere. I'm looking into old unsolved case files in the area to see if anything like this has happened before."

"You don't think this is his first victim?" the sheriff asked.

"I don't know. He bound her and brought her to the river to kill her. He wanted to chase her. Some of it was planned and neat, while some things were left up to chance. Becky was an athlete, and she could have outrun him. He could have gone through into the water. I don't know if it was planned out exactly as it happened, but I think he's had some practice before. He could have killed Becky in any number of ways, but he wanted her to freeze to death. I really hope there is not another victim, or we might have another serial killer in the area."

"Then we are really glad you are here," the sheriff said.

"How is the family doing?" Kelsey asked.

"Not good, especially after what happened with Simon. Where are we with the alibi?"

"Deputy Gallant is checking into it. Simon claims he has an alibi for the entire night. If it checks out, then maybe the Samson family has a little less pain to deal with."

"Liv and Jess are with them right now. Jess wasn't in as much contact with Becky after Becky moved to Montana for school, but they still kept in touch and would call each other every couple of weeks. I don't know how my daughter is taking this yet, but Liv and I will be there for her when she needs to grieve."

"You need to grieve, too," Kelsey reminded. "From how you talk about Becky, you were a father figure in her life."

"We'll get through this together," the sheriff noted.

Kelsey took some solace in that. Winchburgh went through everything as a community, and they were already coming together to work through this atrocity. The town would never be the same again, but they would heal in time. Kelsey still didn't feel like a local, but she wanted to help with the healing process.

The door opened, and John stormed in, hanging his hat on a hook and tossing his jacket on another. He looked ready to snap.

Kelsey looked over at him, hopefully.

"The alibi checks out," he said. "Simon was with friends until around midnight, nowhere near the river, and all of their stories match. He took a girl home that night, and she has given a statement confirming that. We also have statements from both housemates confirming Simon came home with a girl and slept late the next morning. I have a couple of officers going through each statement again with the witnesses, but I don't think anyone is lying."

"I'm going to pay the Samsons another visit and pick up Liv and Jess. I can let them know that their son is not a suspect anymore," the sheriff said.

"Not a killer, but he's getting into other stuff." John looked back at Kelsey. "We found the package he tossed from his snowmobile: cocaine. He didn't murder his sister, but he is dealing stronger stuff. We still have him in the station."

Sheriff Anderson sighed. He looked at Kelsey.

"It's your call," Kelsey said. "The family is going through a lot of pain."

"Everyone goes through some pain," John snapped.

Kelsey and Sheriff Anderson looked over at him—a storm was brewing on the deputy's face. John shook his head and opened his laptop, bashing on the keys. His regular office was back in the police station, but he had taken a desk in the FBI office while working with Kelsey on the current case.

Sheriff Anderson gave Kelsey a look: *I have other things to deal with, so he is all yours.*

"They are going through a lot of pain," the sheriff confirmed. "I'll speak with Simon and hopefully talk some sense into him. He knows we have him bang to rights, but you didn't see him toss the drugs, did you?"

Kelsey shook her head.

"So, we let it slide for now, but remind him that we don't hold back if we catch him doing anything like this again. I don't know if the Samsons can grieve together, but I want to give them a chance."

"I'm still on reasonably good terms with Ernest," Kelsey reminded. "If Simon and his buddies are moving cocaine, they are stepping on the toes of the bikers. Get in too deep, and they are not going to like that. Let me know when you have spoken to Simon, and I'll ask Ernest to send someone over to give the boy a scare. Hopefully, that dissuades him from going down the wrong path."

The sheriff nodded and gave a sly smile. "You're fitting in well here, Hawk."

Kelsey waited until the sheriff was gone before she dealt with John.

"Care to tell me what is going on?" Kelsey asked.

"Huh?" John threw back, glancing up over his laptop.

"You stormed in here like someone punched you in the face on the street. What's got you so riled up?"

"We're chasing a killer who might strike again. One of our own was murdered right here in town. And I have to deal with her asshole brother giving me crap because I'm trying to do my job. What part of that is supposed to make me cheerful, Hawk?"

When the sheriff called her Hawk, it was a term of endearment, but it felt different coming from the deputy. Kelsey stood up and walked over to the deputy's desk.

"We are both investigating the same case, *Gallant*," she snapped back. The search for similar cases was not fruitful, which was why Kelsey was so irritable. "I'm not happy, too, but I don't come storming in here with an attitude. I've seen you handle crap like this, and you always have it together. I know you are riled up with this case, but we can't work together if you are going to be like this. So, care to tell me what is really bothering you?"

John's finger hovered over a key, and his other hand tensed into a fist. Kelsey was not scared that he would lash out at her, only that he would not be honest with her. He stared at his screen and breathed for ten seconds before regaining composure.

"Samantha wants to go to counseling," John said plainly.

"Your wife?"

"Yeah, she thinks we are having marital problems."

"She said that?" Kelsey asked.

39

"She didn't say it like that, but she did mention that it might be helpful and that we could benefit from talking with someone together," John replied.

"That's not a bad thing, John. It shows she cares. If she thought there was a problem and didn't do anything, that would be the time to worry. She wants to be with you, so let her help."

"Says the woman who was cheated on by her last befriend," John snapped.

Kelsey was over that relationship, but hearing John speak about her relationship like that still hurt. She stared down at him and waited for him to apologize. He did a minute later when he shook his head and grimaced.

"Sorry, that was uncalled for," John said. "I just don't know why we can't figure this out by ourselves. Why do we need someone else to come in and tell me everything I'm doing wrong?"

"Are you doing anything wrong?" Kelsey asked.

"I'm not perfect," John said. "No one is, but I can fix it."

"Like you fix things in your job."

"Maybe that's why it feels so futile. When I come to work, and there is a problem, I go out and fix it. With my marriage, I don't know what to do. I feel so lost, and it really sucks."

"Winchburgh had a serial killer, and you were all in over your heads. I don't mean that as an insult, but it's true. I was here to help, and I was trained in how to catch him. When you can't do something by yourself, you call in a professional who knows what they are doing."

"Yeah, I get that, but—" John balled his fist again and pushed it into the desk. "I see what you are doing, Hawk. Yeah, you are right, and my wife is right, too, but that doesn't make me feel any better. Stop trying to psychoanalyze me. You might be the expert in this room, but you're not a therapist."

"Yeah, I'm not," Kelsey agreed. She wasn't in any position to give out marriage advice. "Just be open to trying things. It's better to solve a problem before it arises, right? We're not waiting around for this guy to kill someone else—we'll catch him before he strikes again."

"Yeah," John sighed. "And I know I'll go to therapy with my wife; it just feels like I'm in the wrong."

"I get that," Kelsey sympathized. "No one likes to be in the wrong, but we all are at some point in our lives. And if you *are* in the wrong, you do what you can to make it right."

John let out a long sigh through his nose. "Can we put whatever this is on hold for now? I like working with you, Kelsey, but I don't want to discuss my marital problems. How about we just focus on the case?"

"Sounds good to me, but I am here for you, John. If you ever need to talk about anything, I'm a pretty good listener."

"You really are fitting in with our community, Special Agent Hawk, and it is so annoying." John smiled.

Kelsey smiled, too. Cases like the current one always weighed heavily on her, and it was nice to work with someone else.

"I've been looking into any older cases with signs of suspicious death. Nothing has popped up from Winchburgh or the surrounding area, but there are some similar cases near the southern state line where someone froze to death."

"What about accidental deaths?" John asked.

"I will circle back to that when I get through everything suspicious in the state. What are you thinking?"

"There was a death in Winchburgh about nine months ago, right at the end of the previous winter. We looked into it, and it was ruled as accidental. Another young woman, maybe eight years older than Becky. She was found in a field on the west side of town wearing skimpy clothes, but there was no sign of any foul play. Officially, she froze to death. I know the family and spoke with them, but there were no leads, and nothing pointed toward it being anything other than an unfortunate accident."

"I want the case file, and I want to know everything you remember about the case. It might be a dead end, but it feels too similar. I also want to talk to anyone who knew Becky Samson at university. I don't want to go to Montana, but we might have to. In cases like this, it's often someone the victim knew. Doesn't feel like that is the case to me, but we have to go in that direction first while working all the angles. If it *is* someone the victim knew, the case becomes a lot simpler. If we find this second case is murder and not accidental, we have a problem. Either two women were killed by someone they knew, and we have two local killers, or we have a potential serial killer on our hands. Our best-case scenario is that a local girl accidentally froze to death. The way I see it, the case is lose-lose no matter the direction."

CHAPTER EIGHT

"Hello?"

"Is that Denise Higgins?" Kelsey asked down the phone.

"Yes, who is this?"

"Special Agent Kelsey Hawk. Do you mind if I ask you a few questions about Becky Samson?" Kelsey asked.

John glanced at her out of the corner of his eye as he drove. They had spoken to half a dozen students in quick succession at the same university as Becky Samson and had come up with nothing so far.

"Is it true?" Denise asked. "Was she murdered?"

"I just need you to answer a few questions for me, Denise. can you do that?" Kelsey pushed.

"I can't believe it. She was such a sweet girl—who would want to hurt her?"

"Were you close to her, Denise?"

"We were best friends. I met her at the student mixer on my first day, and we have hung out almost every day since. I don't understand how this happened. Who did it?"

"Did she have a boyfriend?" Kelsey asked, hoping to get something from the woman who was closest to Becky.

"No, never a boyfriend," Denise continued. "She would make out with guys at parties sometimes, a girl once, but she always put her studies first. She told me she didn't have time for a boy."

"Did anyone take an interest in her? That might have been frustrating if someone liked her, but they were turned own," Kelsey said.

"Oh, my goodness! Was it someone at the school?"

"You are perfectly safe, Denise. I only want to get a feel for her life, okay? Was there anyone who was around a lot? Someone who might know her as well as you do?"

"No, I don't think so," Denise sobbed.

"You are doing great, Denise. Everything you are telling me is being very helpful. How about her grades? Did she do well in school— had her grades dipped recently?"

"No, she was always near the top of her class, and I think her grades improved in the past semester. I was a little jealous of her. Oh, no! I don't mean like that."

"You really don't need to worry, Denise," Kelsey said. "You are not a suspect, okay?"

Kelsey knew that everyone was a suspect until they were ruled out, but telling people that didn't do anything when trying to get answers from them.

"How about her behavior?" Kelsey continued. "Did it change at all over the past semester? Did you see less of her? Could she have been seeing someone without you knowing it?"

"No, she was the same as always. We share a dorm room here." Denise suddenly went silent. "*Shared.* I can't believe she is gone. Sorry, I want to help. There was no change, nothing. I saw her every day, and we always hung out. She wasn't seeing anyone, I know that. Although, there was one guy. I don't know, I think he was a teacher from when she was at school. He came looking for her, but she was on a field trip. I never saw him again. He was just passing through."

"Do you know his name?" Kelsey asked.

"No, he didn't say anything other than he knew her from school, but he was much older than her, so I figured he was a teacher."

"When did he visit?"

"Maybe a month ago. Becky wasn't sure who he was when I mentioned him. I didn't figure it was very important," Denise said. "I should have said something to the police."

"It is probably nothing, Denise. They couldn't have done anything anyway, alright? Just in case, I'm going to have you call someone at our office and give them a description, okay?"

"Okay," Denise responded.

"When was the last time you saw Becky?" Kelsey asked.

"It was a week ago. She told me she was going home to surprise her family."

"Did you believe her?"

"Yes, of course. She did that every so often. She wouldn't lie to me about that; she wouldn't. She packed her bag, and I didn't see her again when she left for the bus. I'll never see her again."

"Are you getting help at your school?" Kelsey asked.

"We have a counselor," Denise replied.

"Good, talk to them, okay? I know this is hard, but you will get through this."

"Please catch them," Denise said. "Please."

Kelsey gave Denise contact information to call and give a sketch of the man who had visited. It was the best lead they had. Everyone had said much the same thing: Becky was wonderful, and no one would ever want to hurt her.

"We need to check bus depot cameras and ticket sales," Kelsey said. "I want to know if she made it back to town or if he picked her up somewhere else. She was on her way back to surprise her parents."

John nodded. There was nothing else to be said. A young woman doing well at school with lots of friends had been murdered when all she wanted to do was go home and see her family. The world didn't make a lot of sense.

For now, she had to think about this new case. Or the old case, depending on how you looked at it. She didn't know what she wanted the coroner to tell them. That she had found new evidence on the body or that it was definitely an unfortunate accident.

Whenever Kelsey liaised with a coroner, she always thought of her mom. She knew her mom as a mother but not as a coroner, but every time she spoke to one about a dead body, she couldn't help but think about what her mother would say in the same situation. From former colleagues Kelsey had spoken to eight years ago, her mother was competent. Most coroners were competent, but some were better than others. Was her mother better than average? Would she help to crack the case if she was helping Kelsey? Had her mother and father ever worked on a case together?

Maybe that has something to do with it.

Kelsey made a mental note to check her father's case files and find out if her mother had ever consulted on a case. If they had worked together to put someone in jail, that could be a reason for retribution.

"She was found in a field," Kelsey confirmed. "Where?"

"On the Gibson farm," John said as he drove them to the coroner's office. "She was found smack-dang in the middle of the corn field, face down in the snow. She froze to death out there."

"And she was wearing skimpy clothing?" Kelsey asked.

"She was, but that was not suspicious. It was the end of winter, and the local kids always have a big barn dance at that time of year. They rotate between the local farms, the ones with a big enough barn, and the kids do fundraisers to raise money for food and drinks and bring in big patio heaters to warm the place—they don't need many by the time they pack everyone in there and get the dancing going. It can get pretty rowdy, and they go late, but they are always far enough away from the town center that they don't create a disturbance."

Kelsey took a breath. "She was older than Becky. What, twenty-seven? Was it normal for someone that age to be there?"

"It was mostly teenagers, ranging from sixteen upwards, but there were older kids, and if you had been before, you were always invited back. Cecily Brown had been going every year from what we know."

"And she was from the community?" Kelsey probed.

"Worked as an accountant in the middle of town. She wasn't born in Winchburgh but grew up not far from here, and her family moved into town when she was still in school. Not much to tell apart from that. She was a quiet girl who kept mostly to herself. She liked to go out and party but wasn't the partying sort. She would have a drink and mix with others but wouldn't go crazy."

"Had she been drinking that night?" Kelsey asked.

"From what I remember, there was some alcohol in her system, but not so much that she would be unsteady on her feet or anything like that. We spoke to people at the barn dance, and there were lots who remembered her there, but no one is sure what time she left. She was found the next morning in the field when it got light. Our best guess was that she left the party sometime after 11 pm and was walking home. We don't know what happened after that, but the cause of death was freezing."

"How far from the barn was she?"

"I would guess about a quarter mile, going by the size of the fields."

"No one saw anything suspicious? No one saw her leave?"

"No," John replied.

"Did she have a boyfriend?"

"No, no boyfriend. Or no boyfriend that we knew of."

"How far was her house from the barn?"

"A couple of miles."

"Do you know how she got to the dance?" Kelsey asked.

"She got a ride from some friends. They had planned to give her a ride home, but they couldn't find her when the party finished around 4 am, so they presumed she had gotten a ride from someone else or hooked up with someone."

"What does your gut say? Would she have tried to walk home from the barn?"

"No, she wouldn't," John confirmed. "That bugged me at the time. It would have been much easier if there had been a reason for her to be in the cornfield. Anyone who lives through a couple of winters here knows not to be outside for long without the proper clothing. And she was going the wrong way if she was going home. There was a dirt road that led back to town that would have been the quickest route. It didn't make sense at the time, but thinking back, it would make more sense if this was the same guy."

"How about shoes?" Kelsey asked. "Was she wearing shoes when you found her?"

"I don't remember. The coroner will know." He pulled up outside the stone building, and the two of them exited the vehicle.

They had called ahead to inform the coroner they were coming, and she was waiting for them in her office. She smiled pleasantly as soon as they entered and invited them to sit down. She had two files on her desk.

"I can show you Becky Samson's body, but we can't do the same with Cecily Brown," the coroner said.

Cecily Brown had been buried a week after she had died.

"What can you tell us about the recent victim?" Kelsey asked,

"You were right about the marks on her shoulders. When we looked closely, there were definite finger marks on the skin but no fingerprints. Whoever did this wore gloves. They applied force to her shoulders at some point close to her death. Your theory about her not being stuck in the ice is also supported by the lesions on her leg. She cut her leg repeatedly on something sharp, and it is most likely she could free her leg from the ice but couldn't move from her spot. She was held down and cut herself repeatedly on the sharp ice as she tried to escape. We also have rope marks on her wrists but not her legs. Other than that, there were no other substantial injuries to her body, internal or external. She officially froze to death."

"How about Cecily Brown?" Kelsey asked.

"She froze to death too."

"Do you remember how much alcohol she had in her system?"

The coroner checked the report. "Point zero four. Not enough to make a real difference in her death or decision-making."

"How about shoes?" Kelsey asked. "Was she wearing any?"

"No, she wasn't," the coroner replied. "It's all here in the report, and there are photos of the body, too." She pushed the file over to Kelsey. "I checked the body at the time and went over the photos after you called, and there are no marks on the body. No sign that she was held down or forced to do anything."

Kelsey opened the file and looked over the photos. There were no marks on the shoulders.

Deputy Gallant's phone beeped—he had been waiting for the case files to be sent through by Marcy.

Kelsey found a picture of the feet. They were bare, with slight blistering on them, but not as much as on Becky's feet. Although, it did mean she had walked or run for some distance.

"Do we know where the shoes were found? Or if they were found?" Kelsey asked.

The coroner shrugged.

"Hold on, I have the files now," John said. "Let me see if I can find anything."

Kelsey went through the reports to see if there was anything out of the ordinary, but she was at a loss. Cecily had left the party at some point and ended up in a field barefoot, but there was no sign she was physically coerced.

"The shoes were found in the morning about twenty yards from the barn. There was nothing suspicious about them, and they were swabbed for forensics, but nothing useful came back. What do you think?" John asked.

"It feels suspicious. They both froze to death, and both were barefoot when found. Do you know where her parents live? Are they still in town?"

"They are," John replied.

"I want to speak to them," Kelsey said.

CHAPTER NINE

Kelsey sat in the passenger seat as John drove once again. Not that she wanted to drive—she was quite happy to have the deputy chauffeur her around; he knew the town much better than she did. She could find her way with GPS and was getting to know the area better, but sitting in the passenger seat allowed her to review the case files before they spoke to the parents.

"What did you make of the parents after the death of their daughter?" Kelsey asked. She didn't want to come out and say it, but most people murdered in a small town were killed by someone they knew. Kelsey couldn't be sure it was murder or even the same killer, but she had a hunch it was more than accidental death.

"They were broken up about it, just like the Samsons. It took them a long time to get over it, and I know they are still grieving. I know we have to talk with them, but I don't want to rake up old graves. They need some peace."

"I know, and I want to give that to them, but if this was your daughter, wouldn't you want to know if she had been murdered?"

"Yeah, I would," John admitted.

"There are lots of statements here—you all did a thorough job with the investigation," Kelsey noted.

"I like to think we do a thorough job all the time, but when it is one of our own, we make sure to do it right and spare no resource."

"Statements from all her friends say the same thing," Kelsey thought out loud. "She went to the barn dance with three other people, and they hung out some of the night, but everyone there knew each other, so no one kept track of anyone else during the night. Someone saw Cecily go out for a smoke on at least two occasions, and they couldn't be sure what she was smoking." Kelsey flipped to the tox report. "Nothing in her system except for a little alcohol. She could have gone out for a smoke and left with someone who was at the party?"

"We thought the same when we were investigating the case. There were a lot of people to talk to, and we couldn't account for the exact

48

movements of everyone that night, but no one was suspicious. She could have left with someone at the party, but I don't think we will ever know. No one in attendance remembers anyone suspicious, but no one knew Cecily Brown was missing either."

"What about this? Mrs. Gibson said she was woken in the night by a dog barking. This was around 3 a.m., right before the party was winding down," Kelsey noted.

"We followed up on that. The Gibsons have around a dozen farm dogs. Mr. Gibson went downstairs to check it out, but the barking wasn't from the perimeter of the building, so it wasn't an intruder. He heard it, too, somewhere in the distance. His dogs have full access to the farm and come and go as they please."

"So, one of his dogs could have been barking at the person who took Cecily?"

"It's possible, though it's not unusual for one of their dogs to be barking through the night if a fox is close to the house or they spot a rabbit or any other wildlife."

"Were there any dog prints near to where Cecily was found?" Kelsey asked.

"I don't know. It's not something I remember writing in any of the reports, but it wouldn't make a difference if there were. Those dogs are all over the place day and night, and dog prints are everywhere."

Kelsey sighed. "If any of their dogs were barking, that would have dissuaded someone from staying out there, right? That brings us back to square one unless the dog and the death are unrelated. The dog could have been chasing a squirrel on the other side of the farm."

"It's possible," John agreed. "You ready to do this?"

Kelsey looked at the house through the truck window. "Yeah."

They left the warmth of the truck and ventured the short distance in the bitter cold to the front door. It was the middle of winter, and Kelsey could not imagine being caught in this without the proper clothing—it would not take long to freeze to death.

John knocked on the door, and a middle-aged woman answered a moment later.

"Deputy Gallant," she said. She looked to Kelsey. "And Special Agent... um?"

"Hawk," Kelsey confirmed.

"Sorry, that's right. Special Agent Hawk. You must excuse my forgetfulness. To what do I owe the pleasure, John?"

49

"Can we come in for a moment?" John asked. "We need to speak to you about your daughter."

"Cecily? What happened? Why do you... is this connected to Becky Samson?"

Kelsey wanted to be straight with her. "There is a chance they are connected, but we can't be sure."

"I knew it," Mrs. Brown wailed. "I always knew there was more to this than the police told us."

"The sheriff and his department did all they could at the time," Kelsey replied. "I've looked at the case files and would conclude it was accidental death. It's only with the recent death that it comes to light. Everything possible was done for your daughter, and we will do everything we can now to ensure justice if there is more to this case."

When they entered, Kelsey saw Cecily's father, a middle-aged man, standing in the living room. He looked more troubled than the mother.

"She was the only child we had," the father said. "Now, she's gone."

Kelsey gave everyone a moment to absorb what was going on. She looked around the room to find similar photographs everywhere. There were pictures of Cecily as a baby and others as she grew up and graduated high school. From the looks of it, Cecily had never gone on to higher education and had remained in town her entire life.

Cecily was seven or eight years older than Becky, and they looked nothing alike. If the same killer had targeted both, then he didn't have a type.

"The police took a statement shortly after Cecily's death asking you if you knew of anyone who might want to hurt her. You said at the time there was no one. Has that answer changed at all?"

"No," Mrs. Brown said. "Cecily was a good girl, and everyone liked her."

"She wasn't a golden child or anything, but she didn't get into trouble," Mr. Brown clarified.

"Do you know if Cecily and Becky ever crossed paths? Did they go to the same school? Run with the same friends? Do you know the Samson family at all?" Kelsey was unsure if she wanted a link with the Samson family—Simon, specifically.

Mrs. Brown pulled out a large photo album. "No, they didn't go to the same school. There's Cecily on her first day. Doesn't she look cute?"

"She does," Kelsey confirmed.

"They didn't know each other unless in passing," Mr. Brown said. "We know the Samson family, but not well. They might have crossed paths, but everyone does in this town. She left her jacket at the barn dance. Did they tell you that?"

"Her jacket?" Kelsey asked. She tried her best to look at the photos Mrs. Brown showed her to be polite, but it was information she wanted.

"It's in the reports," John confirmed.

"Why would she leave the barn dance without her jacket and walk into a cornfield?" the father asked. "It doesn't make sense, does it?"

Kelsey knew it didn't, but she had nothing to give them.

"Special Agent Hawk, I know someone did this to my daughter," Mr. Brown said. "I don't care what the police said back then or now. A father always knows. She would not have gone off into the field. She was not that stupid. I want you to promise me you will get this guy, just like you did with the last one."

"We don't know anything for sure yet, but I promise you that if we find out your daughter was murdered, I will get him," Kelsey confirmed. She knew better than to tell a parent that, but she needed to give them hope.

Kelsey looked down at the photo album as the silence descended. "Your daughter was sporty? Did she do track or cross-country?"

"No, she was involved in more team sports. Basketball, hockey in the winter, soccer in the off-season. Only while she was in school, she never kept it up when she graduated." Mrs. Brown flicked through the pictures of Cecily playing sports.

Something caught Kelsey's eye. "That photo," she said, pointing to the team soccer photo. "Can I have it? I need to check something."

Mrs. Brown looked at her husband before slowly pulling it out. "Sure," she said, confused. "What is it?"

"I don't know yet. It could be nothing. John, but we need to go." Kelsey looked back to Mrs. Brown. "I'm going to have an officer come to take another statement if that would be okay with you. Just to double-check everything and to add anything you might want to add."

Mrs. Brown nodded.

"Where are we going?" John asked.

"I'll tell you on the way," Kelsey replied.

***

They pulled up at the Samson house fifteen minutes later. John followed Kelsey from the vehicle as she stormed up to the door and knocked. Mr. Samson opened it.

"I need to check something," Kelsey said, not stopping to remove her shoes.

"What's going on?" Mr. Samson asked.

Mrs. Samson stood up, startled when Kelsey entered the living room. Kelsey did not stop. She held the photo up before her as she searched the wall. She finally found the photo she was looking for and held the photo she had taken from the photo album beside the framed picture on the wall.

"There," she said as John joined her.

John looked at both photos. "They had the same soccer coach."

CHAPTER TEN

"Hey, Marcy, I need you to run a name for me if you can," Kelsey said. "Arnold Sanchez."

"Sure thing, hun. Do you want me to send the details over to you when I have them?" Marcy asked on the other end of the line.

"I'll wait, Marcy. I want to know if he's been in any trouble with the law before, and if not, I need you to find me an address for him."

"No worries. Let me check that right now for ya."

Kelsey could hear Marcy tapping on the keyboard—she was the loudest typer Kelsey had met.

"I don't know him," John admitted. "I'm guessing he came in from out of town or left town a few years back. The face is kind of familiar, but I don't remember ever having a run-in with him."

"Just be ready to go as quickly as you can," Kelsey said.

Marcy finished typing, and there was a satisfied sigh. "Ya, he's in here. We haven't arrested him, but he has been arrested before—multiple times in Vanburgh country. Says here he was released from prison a year ago."

"Give me the last known address, Marcy, and send the rest over to my phone, if you will."

"Sure thing," Marcy replied. "It's an address in Minot. Do ya know where that is?"

"I don't, but I'm with Deputy Gallant, and I'm sure he does. Text the rest of the address with the details, and we'll head straight there," Kelsey said before hanging up.

"Released a year ago from prison, and currently residing in Minot. You up for a road trip?"

"I'm not sure that's a question," John said, starting the truck. "Do you want to liaise with local law enforcement there?"

"Not yet. I don't want anyone speaking to him before we do. If he's our guy, I want to make sure we get it out of him."

"You got it," John said.

They pulled away from the Samson house, and ten minutes later, they were on the highway, heading out of town. Not far outside town,

Kelsey saw the sign for the City of Bridges, where she had finally caught Richard Gibson. It was heralded as a great tourist destination, but Kelsey had not returned since she had plunged through the ice into the water. Perhaps she would pay a visit in the summer.

Kelsey's phone pinged, and she opened up the information from Marcy.

"Shit!" she said.

"What is it?"

"He was released from prison a year ago after serving five years for sexually assaulting a high school student in his position as a teaching assistant. He committed the crime at a school in Dickinson. Do you know it?"

"I know the town, but I've never stopped there. Any more information?"

"Just says that he went into the girl's locker room after a practice and groped an eighteen-year-old student. She told her parents, and they had him arrested for sexual assault. He denies it, claiming she was coming into him. He was supposed to serve seven years but was let out early for good behavior. Before that, he lived in Wilkinson, which I know is not far from Winchburgh."

"You're getting the lay of the land," John noted.

"So, he must have commuted from there to coach soccer when Cecily was in school. After prison, he moved back there, and that's when he would have coached Becky."

"If he were working for the school, they would have done a thorough background check, but he must have slipped through the net somehow. Maybe he used a fake name, or maybe he was part of a group that wasn't vetted."

"He left Wilkinson a couple of months ago to move to Minot. So, he's released from prison, and he comes back to a place that is familiar and a familiar role, too. He coached both girls, and he assaulted a girl around the same age as Becky. Minot is how far from Winchburgh?"

"Three hours," John replied.

"That's an easy commute if he wanted to commit a second murder in an area he was familiar with. So, he coaches soccer, moves to be a teaching assistant, assaults a girl, goes to prison for five years, moves back to where he first coached soccer and kills Cecily. When he gets away with it, he does it again. He thinks he is far enough away that he won't be a suspect. What's his motive? He thinks young women owe him something? No, there's more to it. He purposely made them

54

barefoot. He wanted to chase them. He wanted them to freeze—that part is important to him."

"I hate when you do this stuff," John admitted. "You can get in their heads and think like them."

"Only to catch them," Kelsey admitted. "I can think like them, but I'm nothing like them."

"I'm glad," John admitted.

***

They drove toward the darkness. The snow had been falling in Winchburgh when they left it, but it came down harder as they drove north. The sun descended, too, and it became night before supper time. Kelsey was still getting used to it. She yearned for the long summers and late nights when the sun did not set until eleven. The snow was bearable in daylight, but it became much harder when it was dark and cold. The farther from Winchburgh they drove, the heavier the snow got.

Each highway lane became two long troughs through the condensed snow. The cars filed into single lines, their wheels following the ruts in the road like a train on rails. It was another reason why Kelsey was glad John was driving. She could deal with driving in a little snow, but the roads this far north scared her.

"This is one of the things my wife doesn't like," John said out of the blue.

Kelsey immediately thought his wife was jealous of them spending time together. She gave John space to continue speaking.

"I work too much," he continued. "Even before this case and the last one, I was always at work. I know I should be in the office so much, but I can't help myself and keep telling myself I'm doing a good thing. I know I'm the one who is mostly to blame for where our marriage is at."

"I get it," Kelsey said. "My previous relationship fell apart because of how much I worked. I know I shouldn't work as much as I do and can't help it either. It doesn't matter how much we console ourselves with the fact we are making a difference in the world; the ones closest to us are the people who suffer because of it. I wish I were a different person sometimes."

"Yeah, me too," John said. "We go to our first session next week, and I want to open up about all of this, but I'm afraid I won't be able to."

"You're going, and that's the main thing," Kelsey said. "Your wife will appreciate that. It takes a lot of courage to admit something is wrong and then do something about it."

"Yeah," John uttered, not adding anything more.

They drove on in silence, the falling snow becoming so thick that John had to slow the truck. There was white in every direction, just like there was in all parts of North Dakota. Kelsey wondered what it would have been like if her ex had come out here with her. He liked the sunny climate as much as she did, and he was nowhere near as resilient. Maybe it was a good thing they had ended it in Valleyview—there was a good chance it would have ended in North Dakota, which would have made things much more complicated.

"We're here," John said. "Or almost." He slowed again as they entered Minot and drove down the main highway for a few minutes before he turned off into a residential area. They drove through the rows of houses and out the other side, where only snow and darkness existed. The truck started to rumble as they hit a dirt track. It led them down to a modest-sized house all on its own.

A sedan was parked outside, and there were lights on in some of the windows.

"I don't like this," John noted. "This is the kind of place you see on TV where cops have shootouts with the occupants. We are going to do this nice and slowly, okay?"

"Take the lead," Kelsey said.

John exited the truck, pulling his gun and holding it by his side as he walked up toward the front of the house. Kelsey pulled her gun, too, and followed close behind. The deputy crept up on the full-size window and he peeked through the corner. He turned back to Kelsey and shook his head. She took the second window on the front of the house, checking through the corner. All she could see inside was an empty kitchen—one of the dining chairs had a woman's jacket on it. They went to the front door together and knocked. When there was no answer, John knocked again. There was still no answer. He tried the handle, but the door was locked.

"The back," John said.

He took the lead again, Kelsey following close behind with her gun. No light came from the house at the rear of the building, but light came from the wooden shed. They moved together, flanking the door until they were close enough to get to the door. Kelsey held up her hand as John reached for it; she wanted to see what they were heading into first.

She moved below the small widow and slowly raised her head until she could see inside.

Kelsey saw a woman bound to a chair with a gag in her mouth, her eyes wide.

CHAPTER ELEVEN

The woman looked from the window to the door. Kelsey followed her gaze but couldn't see anyone else in the room. She knew they had to act before something happened to her—Arnold was not in the room with her. She quickly rounded the shed back to the front, pointing her gun at the house. She nodded to John, but it was locked when he tried the door.

Kelsey stood back, her gun trained on the back door—she looked over her shoulder to see John take a step back and then slam his shoulder into the wood, forcing it open. He bundled into the room, and Kelsey followed him in immediately, swinging the door closed so they could not be seen from the back of the house. She did not want Arnold to have a clear shot if he approached the shed.

"You are going to be fine," John said. "I am Deputy Gallant from Vanburgh County, and this is Special Agent Hawk. He pulled the gag from her mouth. "Are you hurt?"

"I didn't sign up for this," the woman said. "I want to leave."

"Don't worry; we will get you out of here as soon as we have dealt with him. Where is he?"

"Arnold?" the woman asked, frightened. "Is this another one of his games?"

Before John could ask anything else, the back door to the house creaked open, and someone descended the steps into the backyard. Kelsey felt a shiver run down her spine. She turned to the woman and placed a finger on her lips.

A high-pitched voice came from outside. "How did you open the door, you naughty girl? You want to play some more games, huh? Well, I've got something you can play with."

The door was pulled open, and Arnold stood on the threshold with a large knife. He was lit from the front, the darkness behind sucking some of the light from the room. He looked from John to Kelsey with confusion. The knife twisted slightly in his hand, reflecting the moonlight—the tip of the blade glinted.

"Drop the knife!" John shouted, pointing the gun.

"You are under arrest!" Kelsey yelled.

Arnold didn't hesitate. He dived to the side so he was out of sight from inside the shed and took off running.

"We're coming back," Kelsey assured the woman quickly.

"No, don't leave me," she pleaded.

Kelsey didn't have time to untie her—she ran out the door with John, chasing down the suspect. There was no bigger admission of guilt than someone running from a crime scene. Kelsey shuddered to think what would have happened if they had arrived any later. What was he going to do to her with that knife? What would he do with the knife now he was on the run?

They didn't need flashlights outside the shed. There was only a half moon, but the snow reflected enough light to see the immediate area, and the track of fresh footprints provided them a trail to follow. John ran with his gun straight out in front of him, and Kelsey followed behind with her gun pointed down in case it went off accidentally. They could not see or hear him yet but would follow the trail for as long as it took.

The only thing Kelsey was worried about was his fitness. He had coached soccer and still looked in shape when she saw him in the doorway. She would not give up pursuit, but he might get away if he had the jump on them in stamina. She also hoped he didn't lead them in a wide loop to get back to the woman and kill her before they could catch him. Or loop back around them to stab them in the back—Kelsey wouldn't hear him coming over the crunch of her and John's boots in the snow.

She glanced behind her even though they were chasing the suspect. The shed with the bound woman slowly receded.

The snow was not as much of a problem for Kelsey anymore. She walked through it every day, and she had gone for some runs in it on the days when the temperature was closer to freezing. She pushed through, keeping up to John.

"Stop running, Arnold!" John demanded.

Kelsey could not see the suspect past John, but he must have caught sight of him. There was no response.

John ducked to the side, diverting his path, and Kelsey did the same. She caught sight of Arnold briefly, the knife glinting in his hand. He could turn and throw it at any time. John would be quick enough to dodge it, but Kelsey would not see it coming.

"Put down the knife, or I will shoot!" John demanded.

There was still no reply.

John motioned with one hand for Kelsey to go left. She did, circling around the left flank of Arnold, and she saw John out of the corner of her eye circling to the other side. John was faster and eventually caught up enough to force Arnold to change direction. When he did, Arnold ran straight for Kelsey.

The ice in her veins was colder than the surrounding snow. Kelsey had faced worse than a man sprinting at her with a blade, but it didn't make it any less terrifying. Arnold's eyes were wide, darting side to side like a wild animal—his knuckles white from gripping the knife tighter.

Kelsey stopped and planted her feet, raising her gun and aiming for his chest. Her heart rate quickened, and she remembered to breathe to steady herself. "Stop, or I will take you down!" Kelsey yelled.

They caught each other's eye, and Kelsey saw the fight in Arnold; he was not a man who backed down. Her finger touched the trigger, steady but ready to pull back. She did not want to shoot him but would not hesitate to do what was right.

She thought he would run straight into her, and her finger slowly pressed the trigger, but he wavered and eventually stopped, skidding in the snow with the knife in front. He raised his hands and turned around, finding John behind him with his gun raised, too.

"Drop the knife, Arnold!" John demanded.

Arnold finally did as he was told and dropped the knife into the snow below.

"I didn't do nothing," Arnold claimed.

"No?" Kelsey asked, breathing normally again. She moved forward with the gun pointed at him, circling around to face the man, ready to kill his next victim. "Then why did you run, Arnold?"

"You were in my shed with guns. I'm not going to stop and ask questions. You sound like cops. I'm not going back to jail."

"That's a matter of opinion, Arnold," Kelsey said, her gun still trained on him.

John moved around to the other side, holstering his gun, and Arnold jerked when his wrists were grabbed, but he didn't put up a fight. John pulled Arnold's hands behind his back and cuffed him.

"How long have you had her tied up?" Kelsey asked as John led him back through the woods by the arm. "How long were you going to toy with her before you made her run?"

60

Arnold snorted. "What? Run where? I was planning on having sex with her."

"You are a sick bastard," John said.

"You don't have a clue, do you?" Arnold asked.

"I know men like you, and you all make me sick," Kelsey said.

"She's a hooker," Arnold said disdainfully.

Kelsey pushed Arnold forward forcefully, and he stumbled and almost fell. "What right does that give you to end someone's life?" Kelsey probed.

"What do you think I'm doing here?" Arnold asked.

"How about you take us through it," John replied, pushing him forward again.

"It's role-play," Arnold continued. "She comes here every couple of days, and I tie her up and pretend to be a home invader or something like that. I pretended to threaten her with a knife, then force her to have sex with me. I mean, I don't *actually* force her. She does it because I pay her."

"She's been here before, and you pay her for this?" John asked.

"You get off on this, don't you, Arnold?" Kelsey was repulsed. "Do you like fantasizing about tying women up and then having them do your bidding? What else do you make her do, Arnold?"

"I don't have to answer these questions. It's not illegal what I'm doing. I pay her for the service, not the sex. It's all above board; you can't arrest me for this."

"How about murder?" Kelsey shouted into his ear. "Can we arrest you for that?"

"Murder?" Arnold asked before growing quiet.

"You were released recently for sexually assaulting a teenage girl, Arnold, weren't you?"

"She was eighteen," Arnold spat back. "I did my time for that mistake."

"So, you admit it was a mistake," John hissed in his other ear.

"Yeah, the mistake was doing it at the school. We were in love, but one of the other kids saw, and when they told everyone, Maria claimed it was assault. It was consensual, and I went to jail for five years. She wrote me when I was in jail to apologize for it. I can show you the letter if you want."

"How about we just untie the woman in your shed first and see what she has to say?" Kelsey asked when they arrived back at it, shaking her head.

When she entered, the woman in the chair started screaming at her unintelligibly.

"Are you a prostitute?" Kelsey shouted above her screaming.

"I won't answer any questions until I have my lawyer present," the woman screamed.

"That won't be necessary," Kelsey said when the woman had calmed down. "We are not here for you." She untied the woman and took out her FBI badge. "Special Agent Hawk. I want both of you in the house now." She glared over at Arnold Sanchez. "We will have a nice little chat about Cecily Brown and Becky Samson."

Arnold's face went white as a sheet.

CHAPTER TWELVE

Kelsey and John followed Arnold Sanchez into his house, with the woman bringing up the rear. He had animal heads hanging on the wall, each one stuck to a wooden shield, looking out at them with glazed eyes. A rifle was hanging on the wall between the kitchen and dining room.

"Do you have any other weapons in the house?" John asked.

"Yes, but only for hunting," Arnold replied.

"Take me to them," John requested. "The weapons first, and then we talk."

"I've done nothing wrong," Arnold claimed.

"Then you have nothing to worry about," John noted.

It was smart to separate them, and Kelsey was glad to get the woman alone. She gestured toward one of the chairs at the dining table, and the woman sat down. She had been confident in the shed but was nervous now and looked a lot smaller.

"How about we start with your name," Kelsey said.

"I don't know what he said to you, but I am not a sex worker," the woman replied. "I will only talk to you when I have my lawyer."

Kelsey sighed and sat down at the table opposite the woman. She looked in her mid-thirties and had a beautiful elegance. Still, the eyes told a different story—one of hardship and learning to cope with the world.

"We can arrange that, but you are not under arrest for anything, and we don't need to question why you are here. All I want to know is if you are here consensually."

"I am," she uttered before falling silent again.

"That's all I care about," Kelsey said. "If you are unharmed, I don't need to ask you any more questions. Depending on what Mr. Sanchez tells us, of course. Until then, we need you to remain here. I will gladly call your lawyer down here if you wish."

"I'm not asking for a lawyer because I've done something wrong. I know how these things go, and I don't want to be tricked into saying anything."

"I get it," Kelsey soothed. "Listen, you are not in any trouble. I am confident that if we looked into you, we would find that you have a reputable business, pay your taxes, and don't exchange sexual acts for money. If we were to dive deeper, we might find you are paid for the role play, and you engage consensually in sex for no money. It might look suspicious, but everything will be above board, and there would be nothing we could do about it. Even with all that, I wouldn't care about your role in his life unless there was more to it than that. We are here for Arnold Sanchez, not for you, okay?"

The woman stared at Kelsey and nodded. The sound of footsteps caught Kelsey's attention as the two men moved around upstairs. It was smart to separate them initially, but Kelsey had not considered that John might be in some danger. What if Arnold pulled a weapon on him? She listened to the footsteps some more, but they sounded calm.

"Virginia White," the woman said.

Kelsey looked back down to the woman.

"That's my name. My legal name. You are right about what you said—if you look into me, you will find nothing illegal."

"I believe it," Kelsey said, happy that the woman was talking. "What does he pay you to do?"

Virginia still looked distrustful and nervous. "He likes to tie me up. He has a lot of fantasies, but the main one is kidnapping. He likes to start outside, sometimes inside. I might be a stranger or a date, and he likes to grab me and tie me up or put a hood over my head. We discuss it all before I come over, and he has never done anything I did not want. When you burst in, I thought he had arranged for something else—it scared me."

Kelsey listened carefully, trying to take it all in while monitoring the other noises in the house.

"It's pretty quiet here," Kelsey noted. "Does Arnold have a dog?"

"No, I don't think so," Virginia replied.

The noise shifted as the two men returned back downstairs. John was holding a pistol and rifle as well as the hunting rifle that had hung on the wall. Arnold looked compliant and composed, and he moved straight to the table, sitting down at an unoccupied side of the table. John took the last remaining side, placing the guns in front of him.

"I have done exactly what you asked me to do," Arnold said calmly.

"I appreciate that," Kelsey said, treating him gently. "Miss White has explained what she was doing her, and I am satisfied that she is not in any danger."

"Before we go any further, I want to clear something up," Arnold said.

"The girl you assaulted," Kelsey noted.

"No, not her. I told you about that already. I made the mistake of thinking she was better than that, but I was wrong. She loved me, too; I know she did, but she was embarrassed of me. I should have ended it before she did what he did, but I didn't assault er. I don't care about that anymore. I was punished for a crime I did not commit, but it is in the past."

"What do you want to confess?" Kelsey asked.

"Clear up," Arnold reminded. "Please don't put words in my mouth. You mentioned Cecily Brown and Becky Samson. I knew both of them—I coached them both in soccer. Cecily was a long time ago, but I remember her. She was seventeen back then, so what is that? Like a decade ago. We had a relationship."

"You had a relationship when Cecily Brown was in school?" Kelsey asked.

"I didn't coach her at school. She took soccer as an extracurricular and always stayed after training. Her parents were always late picking her up, so we talked, and sometimes I would give her one-on-one coaching." Arnold shot a glance at John. "Not like that," he sneered. "It was never like that. We kissed, but that was as far as it went."

"She was a minor," Kelsey warned.

"You are sick," John said. "Were you in love with her too?"

"We were in love with each other."

"You seem to fall in love with children a lot," John noted, sitting a little straighter. His hand was on the rifle, not that he would use it.

"Cecily was not a child. She was two months away from her eighteenth birthday. And the other woman, the one I went to jail for, was eighteen. I'm not a pedophile."

"You were in a position of power," Kelsey noted.

"I never took advantage of that. Ask Cecily."

"Well, that's going to be difficult, seeing as she's dead," John spat.

"What?" Arnold gasped. "Dead? When? How?"

Kelsey let him stew for a few seconds. He sounded genuinely surprised, but he was also a man who liked to role-play. She couldn't tell yet if he was genuine or acting.

"When was the last time you were in Winchburgh?" Kelsey asked.

"I didn't kill her," Arnold said. He thrust his head into his hands. "I loved her."

"When was the last time you were in Winchburgh?"Kelsey repeated.

"I've not been there for months. Wait, you mention Becky Samsom, too. She's not...?"

"Dead," John confirmed. "Another eighteen year old. She was an attractive woman, Arnold. Did you fall in love with her too?"

"No," Arnold said. "Who are *you* attracted to? Do you fall in love with every woman you meet? Or man?"

"What the hell are you talking about?" John asked.

"I fell in love with two young women, but I've loved plenty of older ones too. That is not my type, Deputy Sheriff. I can give you names and numbers of women if you like, and there are ten times more parents I could have had relationships with than their kids. I coached them in soccer, but I didn't kill them."

"Do you have an alibi for the last week?" Kelsey asked.

"I don't know, I'll have to check. I was nowhere near Winchburgh in the last week. What happened to her? How did she die?"

"We are asking the questions, Mr. Sanchez," John reminded.

"I can give you my schedule if it will help," Virginia piped up. "I'm not taking a side here, but I come here a lot, and I want to know if he could have killed her."

"Killed her?" Arnold snapped. "How can you say such a thing?"

"I don't know, Arnold! Some of the things you want to do to me... well, other men do them too, but no one else is accused of murder or has been to prison for assaulting a young girl."

"Woman! She was a woman!" Arnold shouted. "And I didn't assault her. I didn't kill anyone!"

The table was silent as John took the phone from Victoria. He scrolled through it and then leaned toward Kelsey, showing her.

"All right, we are going to need a copy of this and separate statements, but if this is the case, then you have an alibi for when Becky Samson was murdered," Kelsey said.

Arnold let out a happy sigh of relief. "I told you."

"Does this go back further?" John asked.

"I have older records at home," Virginia confirmed.

"We will need them, too," John said.

It clicked for Kelsey that Arnold was the man who had gone to see Becky at her university. She hadn't gotten his name, but her gut told her it had to be.

"It was you, wasn't it?" Kelsey asked. "You went to see Becky in Montana!"

"I... I have an alibi for her death," Arnold stated.

"Did you visit her at college?" Kelsey demanded.

Arnold was silent for a few seconds. "Yes. I was passing through and thought I would see how she was doing."

"See how she was doing?" Kelsey scoffed.

"She wasn't there," Arnold said quietly. "What more do you want me to say? It's not a crime to visit someone, is it?"

"That depends on what you intend to do when you see them," John said, his face red.

Kelsey took a breath and placed her palms on the table. "Cecily Brown died nine months ago." They didn't know for sure that Cecily was murdered.

"I didn't know," Arnold said softly. "I wish I had known. I would have gone to the funeral."

"You were still coaching around that time," Kelsey noted. "You lived close to the town and didn't know she had died?"

"We weren't in contact anymore. We only dated for a short time, and—"

"Don't call it dating," John snapped. "She was a kid, and you were an adult. Those are the facts."

"However you want to put it," Arnold replied. "And, no, I didn't know she had passed. I only came into town to coach, and people don't walk around talking about people who have died."

"Do you know anyone who might have wanted to hurt Becky Samson?" Kelsey asked.

"No, she was a sweet kid and very popular. She was friends with the Sheriff's daughter. I never coached her, but she would watch Becky at the games."

"How about Cecily Brown? Would anyone want to hurt her?"

Arnold Sanchez was not a suspect in the Becky Samson murder anymore, as long as his alibi checked out, and Kelsey had to hope that if Cecily Brown had been killed, it had been by the same person, and they didn't have two killers on their hands.

"No, but I haven't seen her for a decade, so I don't know what's changed since then. She had it tough growing up, and I think she saw me as a father figure. I tried to guide her, and I did hear she was doing okay for herself, so maybe that worked."

"What about her father?" John asked.

"What do you mean?"

"You said that she saw you as a father figure."

"Her father was not around a lot when she was a kid. He was in and out of jail when Cecily was in her teens. It can't have been easy on her mother. I think the mother went through the same thing when she grew up, not having a father around, and history repeats itself, doesn't it?"

"Yeah, it sure does." John leveled Arnold with his gaze.

"We need to take formal statements," Kelsey noted. "I saw a vehicle outside, and I presume that's yours, Virginia?"

Virginia nodded.

"Good. Now, I would like to ride to the local police station in that car with Virginia and have Arnold ride with Deputy Gallant. Does anyone have a problem with that?"

"Am I under arrest?" Arnold asked.

"We only need to detain you until your alibis check out. I don't see the need to arrest anyone."

"Okay," Arnold muttered. He looked at John, a little wary to be riding with him.

"I'm going to need to cuff you," John told Arnold.

Arnold looked from John to Kelsey.

"He knows better than to do anything to you, and I believe you are innocent until something tells me otherwise," Kelsey said.

"She's the boss," John said grimly.

Arnold took a deep breath and stood up for the table, turning around and putting his hands behind his back.

"Let's go," Kelsey said.

She rose from the table and walked out with Virginia while John cuffed Arnold. She did believe Arnold was innocent but would wait for more information to come through before she was sure. She did, however, want to talk with Cecily's father again.

Kelsey was tired—death surrounded her in every direction. She was stuck in town for the night, and having to wait to get back to Winchburgh made her stressed. Her sleep was going to be anything but peaceful.

CHAPTER THIRTEEN

Kelsey walked down the long hallway. One side was covered in an enormous mirror, so she walked side by side with herself. She did not dare look to the side in case it was not her in the reflection, but she kept watch of the mirror in her periphery. The little girl mirrored each step she took.

She was not alone in this place, not only because of the mirror. She had to get to the end of the hallway, to the red room. It took an eternity. Kelsey grew up, died, and was reborn while walking the long corridor. She looked at her feet briefly—black school shoes with a pretty pink bow on the top. She looked straight ahead again. Had the girl in the reflection also looked at her shoes?

The hallway did not have lights, but there was illumination. Ambient light was everywhere, descending into pink as she approached the red room. She only had to keep walking without looking back. Someone was behind her, walking slowly. Kelsey had to remain calm. If she quickened her step, the figure behind, just out of view, would quicken the pace, too, and she would be caught.

Kelsey tried to breathe, but she was unable. She did not need to breathe there—wherever there was. She was almost in the room when the figure walking side by side stopped. Kelsey did not dare stop. The reflection in the mirror might become captured, but it would not get her. She bathed herself in the red light emanating from the room, and when she reached the threshold, the others disappeared: the figure, its reflection, and her reflection. She was alone in the hallway but would not be alone in the room.

"Come in," came the whisper—the voice of her mother. "Come and join us."

Kelsey looked into the room but could not see the figures in the bed. The blankets mostly obscured them, but the light was thickest and darkest near the back of the room—a thick sludge of scarlet illumination. Kelsey did not want to be alone anymore. She stepped over the threshold, knowing there was no going back.

She approached the bed, searching for the eyes of her mother or father, but she did not see them. She only saw shapes writhing under the covers. The blankets were lifted on one side.

"Yes, come in."

Kelsey moved around the bed and placed a hand on the black sheet. She moved onto the bed and lay prone. The blankets fell over her, descending the world into darkness. She felt bodies under the covers: two large and one small. She hoped they were her parents and sister. She had to believe they were. They took her in a loving embrace.

"You are with us now."

Kelsey sat bolt upright in the bed. It took her a moment to remember where she was. The peeling, floral wallpaper brought it flooding back: a hotel in Minot. It had been late when they got to the police station, and neither of them wanted to leave until they had answers. So, they found the best motel money could buy, which was also the worst. Still, the bed was not completely uncomfortable.

She looked toward the curtains that would have done a poor job keeping out the sunlight if the day had dawned. It was pitch black outside, but the humming clock radio by the bed showed 7:04 in bright red numbers. Kelsey glanced to the other side of the double bed to find it empty, just as it had been the previous night. She was thankful that John didn't even joke about sharing a room. Would she have said yes? Her dreams lately had left her not wanting to be alone.

The bed creaked when she sat up and swung her legs over the edge. She picked up the phone from the base and hit 9 to dial out. She tapped in the number she had memorized and waited for it to ring.

"Yeah?" the hoarse voice said with a cough.

"Mr. Waters?"

"You again?" Harvey said angrily. "You using different phones now to try and trick me?"

"No, no tricks. I'm in Minot looking into a murder."

"Yeah? And why would I give a damn about that?"

He wouldn't, and she didn't expect him to care about the case or her dreams, but she needed to feel closer to her parents, and he was one of the few connections to them.

"Did my parents ever work any cases together?" Kelsey asked.

"How would I know?"

He was the one who investigated their murders; he didn't work with them.

70

"I don't know. Sorry, I didn't mean to wake you."

"Well, you did," he said. "Look, you got the right idea about using a different number, but don't call again, okay? If I need to talk with you, *I'll* contact *you*."

"Wait, what—"

The line went dead.

What did he mean by that? Was it not safe to contact him, or had he been impressed by my getting through to him? He wouldn't have answered if he had known it was me. Still, he sounded scared to be talking to me.

Kelsey couldn't help feeling some hope. There was more behind this if there was a reason not to contact him. She knew the hope was the worst, but she needed to have some. She needed to believe she could do something to put them to rest.

The knock at the door startled her, and she glanced at her gun in the holster on the chair by the bed.

"I'm going to get some breakfast," John said from outside. "You want to come? You want anything?"

"Um, yeah," Kelsey said, running her hand through her hair. She approached the door in her underwear. "Where are you going?"

"There's a small coffee place over the road. They probably have some pastries or something. I figured we would grab a quick breakfast and get on the road. Sanchez has an alibi for Cecily's death, too, so there's no point staying here longer than we need, right?"

"Airtight?" Kelsey asked.

"Yeah, looks that way."

"All right, let me get packed up, and I'll meet you over there in fifteen," Kelsey said.

"Sounds good."

Kelsey pressed her back to the door and listened as the footsteps receded. She suddenly felt cold and hugged herself.

Cold everywhere I go!

Kelsey was on her way to the bathroom when she stopped and went to the small table beside the bed. She tossed her holster onto the bed and sat down, grabbing her bag and removing the case files. Soothing was nagging at her. She went through everything as carefully as she could and found it.

***

"Sorry," she said when she got to his table.

"I ordered you a coffee," he said. "What did you find?"

Kelsey chuckled.

"I can see the look in your eye, and there was no reason for you to be late unless you were onto something," John added.

"We are definitely done with Arnold Sanchez?" Kelsey asked.

"Unless multiple people are covering for him. Virginia White confirms she was with him when Becky Samson was murdered, and when Cecily Brown died, he was in Mexico with a couple of friends. No doubt trying to bag himself a Mexican kid at the beach. We've tracked down the ticket sale for Becky Samson to take the bus to Winchburgh, and CCTV shows her getting on the bus. We can track her all the way to Fargo, but she would have taken local buses from there or maybe hitched a ride. We have her in Fargo five days before she was murdered."

"I don't think it will turn up anything, but speak to someone at the bus station and see if they saw her or if someone else was with her."

"You don't sound confident," John said.

"I'm not. I have a feeling she made it into town, and that's when our killer picked her up. Keep talking to people. Someone might have seen something."

Kelsey took a moment. John was a man of principles, and while it disgusted Kelsey, too, it really got to John that an adult had a relationship with a minor. Maybe it was because he had a little girl, and she might have to deal with stuff like that in the future. Maybe it was all the young women being murdered. One serial killer and possibly another, and they both targeted women. That wasn't something that normally happened in this area, but his daughter would grow up in a place where it had.

There would be time to explore that more on the drive home. For now, she had to show him what she had found. If Arnold Sanchez was a dead end, this was the next lead they would follow.

Kelsey sat down and took a sip of coffee before she pulled out the files. She took a bite of one of the apple pies on the plate in the center of the table when her stomach rumbled and started riffling through them.

"This is Mrs. Samson's statement, right?"

"Yeah," John confirmed.

"She doesn't mention it here, but do you remember when we spoke to her, and she told us both her parents died not long after she was born?" Kelsey asked.

"Yeah, I think so." John took a drink of his coffee.

"Well, Arnold Sanchez said something last night that didn't register until this morning. He spoke about being a father figure for Cecily."

"Yeah, I remember that," John admitted.

"And Cecily's mother had gone through the same thing—mentioned that the mother had a father absent from her life and some other stuff about the family. So, it got me thinking about that, and I made some calls while walking over here. Do you want to know what I found?"

"Hit me with it," John said.

"They were both in the same orphanage. Becky Samson's mother and Cecily Brown's mother both grew up in an orphanage not far from Winchburgh. It's closed down now and has been for about twenty years, but it can't be a coincidence."

"Yeah, that's really weird. So, what? Someone is targeting daughters of women who grew up in the same orphanage."

"It sounds insane, but it fits. It could be a coincidence, but it could also be a connection."

"Okay, so what do we do next? We're driving back to Winchburgh, right?"

"We are. I want to talk to both mothers again, and I want to talk to Mr. Brown—find out what he was in jail for. If Arnold Sanchez was telling the truth about that."

"You don't think he did it, do you? He seemed pretty angry about his daughter's death and was convinced it was murder."

"A good place to hide. If he knows we are looking into it, he might think it makes him look more innocent if he seems outraged. The anger could be because he believes his daughter was murdered or because he is a murderer, and the guilt consumes him. Two deaths in the same area suggest it's someone local."

"We should get going now so we can get back and figure this out." John gestured toward one of the baristas, gesturing for a bag to pack up the pastries. He turned back to Kelsey. "What about the orphanage?"

"I've already put in a request for information. There's a chance the killer is connected to the orphanage, maybe someone who worked there. If not, we might be able to protect anyone with a daughter. It will take some time, but we might just save a life."

CHAPTER FOURTEEN

Kelsey sat down in front of Sheriff Anderson. She was tired, but that wasn't going to slow her down.

"What's the update, Hawk?" Sheriff Anderson asked.

"I'm waiting on Deputy Gallant to return from talking with both families again, but I got some information through regarding the orphanage, and it's confirmed that both mothers went to the same orphanage. Not only that, but Cecily Brown's father went there too."

"So, three people involved in the orphanage?"

"I'm classing it as two parties—three people from the orphanage, but two families. Deputy Gallant is checking for any other connections. I also ran Mr. Brown's name, and it turned out he spent some time in jail for auto theft and drug possession around twelve years ago, but he's been clean since then."

"You suspect him?" the sheriff asked.

"I suspect everyone until they are proven innocent, Sheriff. Still, it doesn't seem relevant. He was arrested and jailed for three years over a five-year span when Cecily was in her late teens, but he's been clean since, and you don't jump from theft to murder with a nine-year gap. He's still a suspect, but not due to the jail time."

"And Arnold Sanchez? He's been ruled out?"

"He has. He knew both women and had a relationship with Cecily Brown when she was seventeen, but he claims not to have seen her for ten years. He looked genuinely surprised and sad when he was informed of her death, and he has alibis for both murders. I've informed the police in Minot to keep an eye on him, but he's not connected. He has all the makings of someone who will do something bad in the future, but I don't believe he killed either of them."

Sheriff Anderson looked down at the picture of his wife and children on his desk.

"How's your daughter doing with all this?"

"She's taken it hard. Becky Samson was a good friend, and it was so sudden. I was a mess at that age, but thankfully, she's got it together.

She's tough, and she'll get through this, but Liv is not letting her out of her sight at the moment."

"The orphanage is connected somehow, and if we can confirm people from there are being targeted, then we can put your wife's mind at rest and determine how we protect the next targets."

Sheriff Anderson nodded. "Where are you with that?"

"The information is trickling through, but it will take time. I have a list of names of children who were at the orphanage, and we are slowly working our way through them, looking for people who have families now. The orphanage was closed down suddenly, and what happened to the building after that is murky. There are no original records left, but some older records were sent to another building, so we might be able to retrieve them. If only everything were digitized."

"Ah, you youngsters rely on technology too much. You should be happy that not everything is digital."

"Why are you smiling like that? What do you know?" Kelsey asked.

"The library. They won't have records, but if something did happen to the orphanage, there would be newspaper clippings on microfilm."

It was Kelsey's turn to smile. "You do know microfilm is digitized nowadays, don't you?"

"You don't need to be jealous just because I know something you don't," Sheriff Anderson joked. "Why don't you go down there and take Deputy Gallant with you?" The sheriff looked toward the door before picking up some of the files Kelsey had brought in.

Kelsey looked around to see John. "Hey. Did you find anything?"

"All three confirmed they were at the orphanage when they were younger, mainly between the ages of three and nine, and it was the worst point of their lives. They were happy to get out. None of them really remember each other, even the Browns. They went their separate ways, but the Browns met again at a support group in the area for orphans, and they hit it off and started a family. Mr. Brown confirms everything on his police record and talks about how he has changed since then, confirmed by his wife. All three have alibis for both deaths, although the Browns are each other's alibi. I don't get the sense that any of them would have a reason to hurt their own children."

"Okay, good," Kelsey said. "Do you want to take a trip to the library?"

"The library?" John asked.

"I thought we could go through some of the digitized microfilms and see if there is anything about the orphanage to give us a head start," Kelsey replied.

"Good idea," John said.

The sheriff cleared his throat loudly.

"Did you find something, sir?" Kelsey asked.

Sheriff Anderson shook his head. "Oh, I'm sure I would if I looked hard enough, but you seem to be on top of it. I was looking over this list to see if I recognized any of the names, but I don't. There is a Linda Carlson—Carlson is my wife's maiden name, so maybe someone in the family knows her. I'll follow up in case it's helpful."

"Thank you," Kelsey said. "Not just for that."

The Sheriff gave a knowing smile.

Kelsey got up and left with John, taking his truck to make the short five-minute trip to the public library.

"How are you doing with all of this?" Kelsey asked on the way. "I know your daughter is only six, but it must be tough to investigate this while she is at home."

"Am I that obvious, or are you just that good at detecting what people feel?"

"A little of both," Kelsey admitted.

"Well, I can tell you that when I was transporting Arnold Sanchez to the police station, I wanted nothing more than to take him on a little detour. I know he's not connected to the murders, but he's not innocent. He might have done prison time, but he still deserves punishment for what he did. I don't care how close someone is to their eighteenth birthday; you don't do that kind of thing."

"Hey, I'm with you," Kelsey said. "If we were there for any other reason, I might have suggested it, but when there are bigger fish to fry, you don't concern yourself with the minnows."

"But the minnows are easy to catch… and snap in half." John sighed. "Stop getting in my head. I don't want to think about any of this right now. I wouldn't have done anything to Arnold Sanchez, but it sure would be nice to be in control of something again."

"Like in the army?"

John smirked and glanced at Kelsey briefly. "What are you? My therapist? No, not like the army. Well, kind of. I could control a lot, but there were still lots I couldn't: so much death, meaningless death. I guess not much has changed."

"We can still control the situation," Kelsey reminded. "It might not seem like it, but every step we take, every person we speak to, brings us closer to the truth. I hope with all my heart that someone else is not killed, but what we are doing will stop others from being killed. We catch this psychopath, and we save people. That's our duty."

"I know," John confirmed, bringing the truck to a stop. "Can we go and do our job and get this guy?"

"Lead the way," Kelsey said.

The library was much as Kelsey expected it to be. Rows and rows of books lined white shelves, plush seats allowed people to read while looking out the window at the harsh conditions, and preschoolers peppered a small kid's area. Kelsey and John were shown to the information room, where decade-old computers were ready to be used.

The tall, confident librarian instructed them on how to pull up the microfilms and search through them. It was very different from when they had to be scrolled through. There was an actual search engine attached. Kelsey and John took a computer and started to look through the information.

"Can't we just Google this stuff?" John asked.

"Not if the local newspapers reported on it—they might not have had online editions."

"Look at this," Kelsey said. "The orphanage burned down, and it was suspected arson." Kelsey skimmed through the article. "Suspicious circumstances, but no one was ever arrested for it. It happened about six months after the orphanage was closed down, so no one was hurt. The building was going to be converted into apartments, and there was insurance to cover it, so nothing was ever done."

"Maybe someone holds a grudge," John said. "The article here talks about an investigation into the orphanage not long before it was closed down. There is some speculation about what went on there. Beatings regularly at night, children not allowed to leave their beds if they wanted to go to the bathroom, and freezing conditions in the winter. Jeez, there are some stamens from people who were there, and they talk about huddling together under one blanket to try and keep warm. A child died there, but it was ruled an accidental death. I'd put money on someone having a grudge and burning the place to the ground."

"Maybe," Kelsey said. "It doesn't answer why people from the orphanage are being targeted. Or why their children are being targeted."

"It could still be a coincidence," John said.

"I know, and I'm worried that it is. This is all we have to go on right now, and I don't want to wait until there is another death to try and find another connection."

They sat in silence, and both went through the newspaper articles about complaints from former children who attended the orphanage, but no names were attached. Until Kelsey found one article about a lawsuit.

"This might be something," Kelsey said. "Three years ago, six former residents filed a lawsuit against the orphanage and some of the staff. This is the only article I have found with names attached."

"The Browns or Samsons? The Browns did talk about getting some compensation, but a lawsuit."

"No, they were not a part of the lawsuit. It does mention some settlement was offered, but the six rejected it. I'm guessing that some people took the settlement as a way to move past it, but others wanted to fight. There's no information about whether or not the lawsuit was won, but I'm guessing it didn't. Otherwise, there would be information about it. It's likely the whole thing was buried."

"Does that fit with what we are looking for?" John asked.

"It's a stretch, but maybe," Kelsey replied. "Someone burns down the orphanage, but it's still not enough, and they file a lawsuit with five other people. When more people don't join, they are angered by it and start targeting those who want to live their lives. There's nothing more annoying than people moving past something and living their lives when you can't."

"So, we track down the people on the list?" John asked.

"We track down the people on the list," Kelsey confirmed.

CHAPTER FIFTEEN

John drove them down a long track road that looked like it led to nowhere.

"He's the closest on the list. Wouldn't it be convenient if he was our guy," Kelsey noted.

"It would make sense," John replied. "I don't know the guy personally, but he's well-known in the area. Apparently, he's big into conspiracy theories. He's been arrested about two dozen times for leading protests to bring down the government, local and federal. Is it still a protest if only one person shows up?"

"I don't know. What else do you know about him?" Kelsey asked.

"He was arrested once for making a threat against the state government. This was about six years ago. He mailed a package of Anthrax to the government offices, but it was caught before anyone opened it. The idiot even wrote his mailing address on the envelope."

"A dangerous idiot," Kelsey warned. "People like him don't do things like that through negligence; they do it because they don't care about people coming after them, and that's usually because they don't fear dying for the cause. How long did he spend in jail?"

"Four years," John confirmed. "Apparently, he was a model prisoner."

"He likely felt like a martyr. That would have made him feel good. I've known plenty of guys like this on both sides of the law. Treat them right, and they are no trouble. Make one wrong step, and they become dangerous."

"So, what's the right step with this guy?" John asked.

"I won't know until I meet him, but if he doesn't like the government, he is not going to like the FBI and Sheriff's office turning up on his doorstep. We tread carefully here."

"Was he the one who filed the lawsuit initially?" John asked.

The truck bumped up and down on the packed snow. "No, one of the six, Trevor Goldson, filed the suit."

"And where is he now?" John asked.

"He's currently six feet under the ground. So, if the leader is dead, then a new leader rises and takes up the cause. Maybe they were friends, and maybe he believed the government killed his friend for looking into the orphanage. I don't know. We have to assume that Terrance Knox is angry and motivated. We also assume that no matter how much help we offer in his cause, he will not believe we are there to help him. If he is the killer, we take him down as swiftly as we can. We don't go in there to kill him, but if he is armed, and seeing as we are driving down a very long dirt track, I am motivated to think he is the type of guy who has weapons in the home, then we shoot if we are shot at."

"Do you think it will come to that?" John asked.

"No, but better to prepare for it and bring him in as smoothly as possible. Either way, I want to take him down to the station."

The truck bounced up and down again, shaking the entire cab. No building was visible in the distance, only large clumps of trees.

"Where did you get with the other five people?" John asked.

"Well, as mentioned, one is dead. I have not been able to get in touch with three of them yet, and the one person I was able to speak to on the phone is living in Canada, and she has no family to speak of. But she did have a lot of interesting things to say about the orphanage."

"Go on," John urged.

"She said when Trevor Goldson contacted her five years ago to discuss bringing a lawsuit against the orphanage, she was hesitant. It was a long time in the past, and she knew how these sorts of things went, but he was persistent and called her multiple times, and she eventually caved. She was one of the first to sign on for the lawsuit, but when only four more people joined, Trevor became depressed, and she said he became more robotic and just went through the motions."

"Was he angry at the others for not joining?" John asked.

"If he was, he didn't show it. From what Maria Willcox told me, he became depressed when the lawsuit went nowhere, and he…."

"He killed himself," John finished.

"Yeah. Jumped from a bridge late one night. Ended his life."

John sighed. "Did the lawsuit end with him?"

"I don't know. We are still waiting for the information, but if Terrance Knox took the lead and it still went nowhere, he might be especially bitter that his friend was driven to suicide. *If* they were friends."

"I know that life can be messy, but you've bought too much mess with you, Special Agent Hawk. Life was much simpler before you arrived."

"Yeah, you are probably right about that." Kelsey gave a wry smile. "Thankfully, I am an expert at cleaning up messes. If you want more stories about how life is messy, you should hear some of the stories Maria told me."

John sighed again. Kelsey could tell all this was getting to him— especially when children were threatened. She had seen it on his face in the library when she had read some of the stories, and it was on his face again. He wanted to protect everyone, but especially children.

"Go on," John murmured.

"Are you sure? The reality is much worse than what was reported in the newspapers."

"Hit me with it," John replied.

"I haven't looked at the files yet to see exactly what was contained in the suit they filed, so the stories are only anecdotal. She talked about being forced outside in the cold. She doesn't remember if she was made to go outside without her shoes purposely or if she forgot her shoes or lost them. Anyway, she was outside on at least two occasions in the snow with no shoes on, and she was sure she was not the only one. I only just got here, but I can't imagine the winters were warmer twenty or thirty years ago."

"They were not," John confirmed.

"She remembers being cold in bed and needing to go to the bathroom but being terrified of doing so. She would hold it in as long as she could, but there were times when she wet the bed when she was sleeping, and she would wake to it frozen beneath her. She would be punished for that, too."

"That's horrible," John said as he slowed the vehicle. They were getting close.

"The worst was the dog. The owner had a large Alsatian that he trained as a guard dog. It would attack anyone on his command, and he used to set it on the kids while it was on a chain, and he would let it get close to their faces. She talked a lot about the large teeth dripping with saliva and was sure there was blood in there, too. He would make it chase them, and he would call it off when it almost caught them. They were all terrified of the owner, but they were more terrified of that dog. They told each other stories of kids being devoured by it. I don't think that happened, but something happened there. Thankfully, the dog must be long gone by now."

"And the owner?" John asked as they stopped.

"Still looking into it, but I want to talk to him, either in person or on the phone."

"Could he be the guy we are after?" John asked.

"It would make sense, but he's old now. He obviously hated the kids, but would that drive him to kill their kids? Again, maybe. But he's old, and the women targeted are fit and were chased. It doesn't make sense that he would purposely chase them. If he had another dog, he might have used it, but there was no sign of any dog attacks. I don't like the man, but I don't think he is the killer."

"This leaves us with one of the other employees if the orphanage is the connection. If this was a former resident and they burned down the orphanage, they would go after him, but they are going after residents. It doesn't make sense. I think Terrance Knox is capable of something like this, but it doesn't make sense that he would target the orphans and not the employees."

"Nothing makes sense yet," Kelsey replied.

She was the first out of the truck for the first time since she had arrived in Winchburgh. She stepped out into the biting cold and didn't like the chill but was driven by the need to stop the killer. She had caught Richard Gibson, but he had killed again after they found the first body. This killer would kill again, but they were only one body in for now (they did not know for sure Cecily Brown had been murdered, and if she had been, it had happened long before Kelsey had arrived in town). Kelsey needed to catch him before he killed again.

She needed to find out what happened to her parents, but she was no further along with that either.

The chill was not the only thing in the air. Kelsey's ears perked up when she heard the sound of dogs barking in the distance. This was the only residence in the immediate area, so the dogs belonged to Terrance Knox. They were a theme in this case: dogs had been heard on the night Cecily Brown was killed, and the former orphanage owner used a dog to terrorize the kids.

Is that a connection? Is the orphanage even a connection?

Kelsey looked down at the locked gate in front of them. The chain was thick, but the gate was wooden and attached with regular hinges. They could easily break through it with the truck, but that might spook Terrance, and he would be less cooperative. To hammer home that they were not welcome there, there were signs—not just for them but for everyone.

No Trespassing!

Trespassers Will Be Shot!

Shoot First, Ask Questions Never!

Kelsey looked at them and then at John. "So, we proceed on foot?"

CHAPTER SIXTEEN

Kelsey and John climbed over the gate and drew their weapons. They scanned the immediate area. There were no cameras or intercom, so he didn't know they were coming unless he had set up another boundary alert. Kelsey was sure he had not. A guy like that thought the government was after him, but deep down, they didn't really believe it. Chances are no one ever came down this far—there were no visitors. He was all alone down there—or Kelsey hoped he was.

"We stay close to the main road down to his residence but keep to the tree line. And we keep six feet between us, just in case," John said.

"Just in case he shoots at one of us?" Kelsey asked.

"If we are smart, it won't come to that. I'm taking the lead, and you stay to my right. This means to stop." John raised his fist. "And this means—"

"I know the signals," Kelsey said. "The army and the FBI share many things."

"I'm not going over this to patronize you. This guy is not dangerous, but he will become dangerous if he sees us coming with our guns, especially if he is the killer."

"I understand," Kelsey confirmed. "We are both on edge. You lead the way, and I'll follow your signals.|

John nodded, his breath escaping his lips in large puffs. It was cold, but Kelsey didn't feel it—not as much as when she had first arrived. The cold had been unbearable a few weeks ago, but it was only awful now. She would feel it a lot more if they were not stepping into enemy territory, but her mind was preoccupied.

From what Kelsey had heard about Terrance Knox, she wished he was the killer. He was immediately unlikeable, and she needed to catch this guy as quickly as possible. Threatening the government was one thing, but actually following through and sending deadly poison to someone who might not be directly responsible for your plight was another. If they could take this guy down, and he turned out to be the killer, it would be a big win.

Kelsey knew nothing was ever that simple. The snow crunched underfoot as they moved through it. The road would have been easier to walk on, compacted by the vehicle that had moved back and forth over it. Terrance had a vehicle, but only he had a key to get through the gate.

The dogs continued to bark, getting louder as they neared the house. Kelsey looked through the trees, but she couldn't see the dogs. She worried they were roaming free and would attack John and her when they got closer.

She had seen no smoke coming from a hidden building. Kelsey didn't have much to go on, but from what she had heard about Terrance, she expected him to be living off the grid. People who had a grudge against the government generally didn't pay public companies for utilities. If he were living off the grid, he might rely on a wood-burning fire. Or perhaps he had a generator.

A bird cawed to the right. Kelsey looked to a branch two feet away, just above head height. A large blackbird was perched on the branch. It called out once more before it took flight and left. They moved on in silence, trekking forever through the unforgiving landscape.

Is this why he lives out here all alone? Some previous trauma from being in the orphanage?

John raised his hand for them to stop. Kelsey moved close to the thick trunk of a fir tree. She did not notice if her hands were cold through the gloves. There was a choice between complete warmth and functionality, and when you worked a job where you might need to use a gun, complete warmth wasn't an option. Of course, that also led to quicker loss of feeling, which would remove functionality. Kelsey flexed her fingers when they stopped to keep the blood flowing. For most other things, she could switch hands and put the other in her pocket, but not when it came to a gun.

John pointed to Kelsey's right, gesturing for her to move slowly to another thick tree where the trees thinned out. Kelsey did as ordered, moving slowly through the thick snow until behind the tree. They could have worn white to blend in better with the snow if they had planned better. It was fine in the trees, but as soon as they hit the open ground, they would be sitting ducks in their dark colors.

"The house," John hissed from his tree. He pointed.

Kelsey looked through the trees and saw a white building around a hundred yards away. If she had to guess, she would say that Terrance had painted the building white to blend in with the landscape. Kelsey looked back at John and nodded.

"His truck is there," John said. "Do you see the trees to your right? I want you to move through them and circle around to the side of the house. I'm going to make a run for the shed. I don't want to spook him, but if he is our guy, I don't think he will let us take him alive. We both know that if he dies, a lot of answers die with him."

Kelsey nodded. Maybe it would all go smoothly, and once they got close enough to talk with him, and he would be reasonable.

"On three, all—"

John didn't get to finish. A bullet thunked into the tree he was hiding beside, splintering the bark and sending tiny pieces of wood flying up into the air. John and Kelsey both ducked instinctively, spinning to get get behind their respective trees, putting the large trunks between them and the gunman.

"That was a warning!" Terrance cried. "I could have hit you if I had wanted to."

"You just shot at a law official!" John shouted back.

"Did you not see the signs?" Terrance replied. "You come into my property with weapons drawn and expect me not to defend myself."

"We are not here to cause any trouble, Terrance!" Kelsey tried. "We only want to talk with you."

"If you had wanted to talk with me, you would have come to my front door. Besides, I have nothing to say to anyone. Who sent you here for me?"

"No one sent us, Terrance!" John called.

"The next shot will not be a warning," Terrance called.

Kelsey looked at John, and he had the same thought. They could go and get backup, but that would give him a chance to leave. One of them couldn't go and leave the other to watch his house. It was either all or nothing, and they were not prepared to lose him. Who knew what other ways out of the property there were?

"Three," Kelsey mouthed.

They both got to their feet and ran. Kelsey kept the gun pointed at the ground as she ran to the right as fast as her legs would take her. She moved slightly farther into the trees, so there were more obstacles between her and the gunman, and sprinted for a full twenty seconds before she stopped and pinned her back to a tree. A gunshot rang out, the same rifle as before, but it wasn't for her. Or if it was, it was wildly off target. There was no thunk into wood or whoosh of a bullet passing close.

Kelsey peeked out from behind the tree at the house, but there was no sign of Terrance. She scanned the windows and both sides of the house but could not see him. She looked over at the shed, hoping to see John pinned behind it, but there was no sign of him either. He would not have had time to run to the shed and then the house. She scanned the ground for his body, but there was nothing.

Kelsey took three deep breaths and took off at a sprint again. She ran through the trees, expecting a bullet to whizz by at any moment, but there were no more shots. He had heard both their voices, so he knew two people were out there. When she thought her lungs would explode, she stopped and hid behind another tree. She was at the side of the house and could see in front and behind it but could not see the doors from her vantage point.

It was eerily quiet in the white landscape—the dogs did not bark anymore. Kelsey waited, taking slow breaths to calm herself, ready to run again. When she was ready, she looked out from behind the tree. She ducked behind quickly when she saw Terrance Knox leave from the back of the house. He was carrying a shotgun. The quad by the large workshop at the back of the house caught her attention. That's where he was going, and if he got out into the wilderness, they might lose him forever.

Kelsey made the decision in an instant, knowing it was the right one to make even if everyone would tell her it was the wrong decision. She moved quickly out of the trees, the gun raised in front of her. She didn't say a word, the crunching of the snow under Terrances's large boots masking the crunching of her footsteps.

"Drop the gun, or I shoot!" Kelsey called.

Terrance spun around. If he were not holding the shotgun in one hand, she would have taken him down, but her instincts told her she had a second to take the shot if he did try to point the gun. Terrance raised his hands to his side, holding the shotgun in the middle. He slowly turned to face her, and his eyes flicked to the side—Kelsey saw it in her periphery. She thought it was John running at them, but it was not.

The dog was snarling and growling as it bounded toward her, teeth bared. Kelsey swung the gun and pointed, but it was different. The dog didn't want to harm her; it had been trained to protect its master. Still, it was the dog or her. She fired the gun, purposely missing and hoping it would be enough. The bullet sunk into the snow, but the sound of gunfire was enough to stop the dog in its tracks with a whimper. It skidded to a stop and backed away, scared.

Kelsey knew it was a mistake and could feel the shotgun pointed at her before it was fired. The gunshot scared her as much as her gunshot had scared the dog, but it didn't scare the dog coming from the other direction.

No! Not a dog!

John slammed into her, knocking the air from her lungs. They slammed into the ground, the shotgun blast missing them. Kelsey was winded, but John was on his feet in an instant. He didn't have his gun, but that didn't stop him from running at Terrance, who still had one shotgun shell in the gun.

Kelsey didn't have to breathe to act. She still had the handgun clamped in her glove and raised it quicker than Terrance could point the shotgun at John. She let her instinct aim for her and squeezed the trigger without the customary exhale. Terrance spun and fired the shotgun, the area echoing with the noise.

Terrance Knox crumpled to the ground, and John was on top of him, taking the shotgun from his hands and searching him for weapons. Blood stained the snow below, thankfully not John's. Kelsey finally regained her breath, getting to her feet with the gun trained on Terrance.

Terrance Knox lay wide-eyed, staring blankly up at the clear blue sky above.

CHAPTER SEVENTEEN

"Where are we at with Terrance Knox?" Kelsey asked.

If they lost him, they would lose any knowledge he had about the killings. Kelsey didn't like loose ends, and if they had the killer, Kelsey needed to know the why behind it. Stopping him was the first priority, but she didn't want him to have an easy way out—he deserved to be punished.

"They are patching him up now. That shot was pretty good—in one side and out the other. He's going to be in a lot of pain for a while, but he'll live. I must thank you for saving my life. Something tells me this will not be the only time you will," John replied.

"Let's call it even. If you hadn't knocked me out of the way, he could have killed me."

"Hey, who knew you could be such a soft touch at heart? I saw you hesitate. That dog was as big a threat as Terrance was, and you chose not to kill it."

"The dog was innocent in all of this. Another dog."

"What are you thinking?" John asked.

"I don't know. The threads are all loose. We still don't know if the orphanage is the connection, and I don't know if dogs are connected somehow, but I think they are. Is he reliving his trauma by chasing the girls with dogs? He was made to be out in the cold, maybe without shoes, and had to live in awful conditions. Maria spoke about being chased by the owner's dog. Right after this, we go and speak with the owner, but if Terrance is our guy, he could be using his dogs to chase the women. Making them go through what he went through."

"Why the daughters of women who used to be at the orphanage?" John asked.

"I don't know, but if the orphanage is the connection, we know those who went there are being punished. Maybe the daughters are a coincidence. If Terrance is targeting people for not joining the case against the orphanage, he might want to punish them in any way he can."

89

"Reverse orphans," John offered up. "Leave the parents without any kids?"

"No, he would have targeted John Samson, too, if that were the case. We need more, but to get more, we need another victim, and I won't let him kill again."

"So, how do we know where the threads lead us?" John asked.

"I hate to say it, but we rely on our guts. We look for what doesn't feel quite right and follow that."

"Don't let the sheriff hear you say that," John noted. "He's stressed enough as it is without you telling him there are no concrete leads to follow. He is doing what he can, though. He found out where the former owner is and texted me the address."

"Good, he needs t—" Kelsey stopped when the doctor exited the room. "Hey, is he awake?"

"He needs some rest," the doctor said.

Kelsey looked down at his name tag: *Jamestown Infirmary. Dr. Weston.* They had to transport the suspect to one of the larger towns to be treated. Kelsey would have loved to have taken him to Winchburgh jail and had him sit in there bleeding out from the bullet wound, but this was the best she would get.

"Is he awake?" Kelsey asked.

"He is, but I can't let you go in there and question him, or there's a threat his blood pressure will elevate, and there could be complications. I don't like it as much as you, but I'm just doing my job. Everyone deserves care."

"I don't disagree with you," Kelsey said. "I'm only doing my job too. Would you like to hear how that is going? Two young women are dead, and more will die if we don't stop whoever is doing it. The man in there, the man who shot at and tried to kill an FBI agent and a deputy sheriff, might be the murderer, or he might hold the key to the case. If you stand in my way, there will certainly be trauma in this hospital tonight. Do I make myself clear, Dr. Weston?"

The doctor sighed. He looked at the chart in his hands one more time as if he were considering it and not delaying to save face. "Just be gentle with him."

"I don't have any other setting," Kelsey replied.

She could see John smirk and almost laugh at the rebuttal.

Kelsey and John walked between the two local police officers who were stationed at the door. Terrance Knox was cuffed to the bed in the small room. He lay with the same expression as when he had laid in the

90

snow. The blankets were pulled down to his stomach, and his left shoulder was bandaged. His eyes flicked to them when they entered.

"Have you come to finish the job?" Terrance asked.

"You have no idea how much I want to do that," Kelsey replied.

"I thought you were supposed to uphold the law."

"You tried to kill me, Terrance. You tried to kill Deputy Galant, too. You are going to jail for a very long time, so how about you cooperate with us, and we can see if we can be a little more lenient? You will get the longest sentence possible, so it is in your best interest to talk to us."

Terrance leaned to the side and sat over the side of the bed. "Yeah, cooperate with those who want to take control of everything. I learned the hard way, but at least I learned as a kid. Most people don't learn this stuff until it is too late. I'm not going to shut up about it. Everyone will know."

"The orphanage, right?" Kelsey asked.

She sat down when John brought her a chair. He positioned one on the other side of the bed, choosing the side where Terrance's hand was not cuffed to the bed.

"Why don't we start there, Terrance? You were at the same orphanage as two of the victim's mothers and one of their fathers."

"The victim's mothers and fathers? What are you talking about?" Terrance asked.

"You know exactly what I am talking about, Terrance. Are you angry about the lawsuit?"

"I'm furious about the lawsuit," Terrance replied. "It's not just the orphanage, you know that, right? It's all the institutions out there. They are all created to cage us."

"Why not the owner, Terrance? He was the one who terrorized all of you, right? Why go after the former residents and not the owner?" Kelsey asked.

"What former residents? Why would I go after the owner?" Terrance laughed. "He's just a man. Put anyone in that seat of power, and they will do the same thing. You don't understand, do you? None of you understand anything, and you are all a part of it. You think you are helping people, don't you? You're just a bar in the cage. You help keep everyone trapped, and you don't even know it."

"The orphanage is where it started, isn't it?" Kelsey tried again.

"You don't understand," Terrance muttered.

"I'm talking about the control, Terrance. It was government-run. They knew what was happening there, but they didn't stop it. You are right not to trust the government."

Terrance's eyes lit up, but he kept himself quiet, no matter how excited he was. "Maybe you know one thing, but there is more to this than you know. I know something you don't."

"Will you cut the crap," John demanded. "I'm sure you know a bunch of things we don't know, and you are more enlightened than the rest of us, but we need answers. I want to know why you killed Cecily Brown and Becky Samson."

"That's why you came here? You want to pin two murders on me? You cops are all the same." Terrance turned his head so he was looking away from John. His eyes lit up some more, and he turned back to face him with a wide smile. "Cecily Brown. Her parents wouldn't sign. They took the composition instead. The same with Becky Samson's mother. They are all sellouts. You think I murdered two women because of the lawsuit, don't you?"

"So, you know them?" John asked.

"I know everyone who didn't sign. I have all of the names burned into my brain," Terrance replied.

"And you hate them, don't you?" John asked.

Terrance looked John in the eye. "With a passion."

"Enough to kill them?" John pushed.

"Almost certainly," Terrance replied.

John looked over at Kelsey. She didn't say a word—Terrance was playing with them. He did hold anger in his heart, but he didn't kill them. He was far too angry at the people who had put him in the orphanage in the first place and then kept him there. That was why he had been targeting the government. He might be going about it all wrong, but he wanted change. He wanted to change the world so other people wouldn't have to go through what he had gone through, even if that meant hurting people—the right people.

"Go on them," Terrance goaded. "Ask me the question you are dying to ask. If you ask it, I promise to tell you the truth, but I find that most people have a hard time listening to the truth."

"Terrance Knox, did you kill Becky Samson and Cecily Brown?" John asked.

"No, Deputy Gallant. They were killed by a ghost. Tell me one of your dark secrets, and I will tell you one of mine. You must have seen some terrible things in war. Aren't you angry at the government for sending you over there? Lots of ghosts over there, marine!"

"I'm done with this," John snapped. "This guy is full of crap. He's going to jail, so either the killings stop, or they don't, and we know it's not him."

"The killings will never stop," Terrance said.

John grabbed Terrance's shoulder and pushed a finger onto the wound. Before Terrance could cry out in pain, John clamped his other hand over Terrance's mouth.

Kelsey was on her feet almost as quickly as John was. She rounded the bed and grabbed his arm. "John," she hissed.

John took stock of himself and let go of Terrance's shoulder immediately. He removed his hand from Terrance's mouth and stormed out of the room, and Terrance burst into fits of laughter.

"I will leave him alone with you in here if you continue with that," Kelsey warned.

"You know I didn't do it," Terrance replied. "I can see it in your eyes."

Kelsey thought about what she had told John before entering the room. They needed to go with their gut, and her gut told her that Terrance was not the killer. And John was right. If he was the killer, he was cuffed to a bed and would be incarcerated when he was healthy enough. After that... Kelsey hoped he could get some professional help.

"You are going to prison," Kelsey noted. "You know what is happening is not right."

"Sacrifices have to be made," Terrance said.

Kelsey could see him waver. Terrance was fighting authority, the people who had wronged him, but he knew innocent people should not be killed.

"Who could be doing this? It's someone connected with the orphanage, isn't it?" Kelsey asked.

"You're wasting your time being in here with me when you should be out there chasing a killer, detective."

"Give me a name. Was it one of the staff? Who was the worst?"

"Oh, the owner was the worst."

"Him and his dog?" Kelsey probed.

"They were both evil. You saw it in my dogs—they are good, but his dog was not. It was not only trained to go after the kids; it wanted to. It had a bloodlust unmatched by his master. What I wouldn't have given to have had him alone without the beast." Terrance smiled and licked his lips. "I would have slit his throat, but I would not have dealt with the beast. It devoured children."

"When you want to cooperate fully, give me a call," Kelsey said.

"I won't ever cooperate with you, detective. It is far too much fun not to. What are you going to do? Offer me a shorter sentence? What you don't understand is that life is a jail. I don't fear being locked up; I already am. Now, off you go and try to do your job. I wish you the very best."

Kelsey tried to hold in her anger as she exited the room so she would not give Terrance the pleasure of seeing the effect he had on her. John was waiting for her outside, fury on his face.

"Well?" John asked.

"He knows something or thinks he knows something, but he won't give it to us. He doesn't care if he goes to jail; we don't have any leverage. He went to jail before, and he became a martyr. He'll do the same again and enjoy every moment of it. Especially when he tells everyone he is in for trying to kill an FBI agent and a deputy sheriff. We'll return to him later when I figure out how to take away his power, but for now, we need to pay the former owner a visit."

CHAPTER EIGHTEEN

"When is the first rehearsal?" the young woman asked.

"I think we are supposed to be there for four, and practice starts at four fifteen," her friend replied. "I don't know why we have to practice; we are so going to win."

The young woman slapped her friend on the arm. "Megan, we only got in because we were the only school band in the area. Do you remember last year when we finished dead last?"

"Yeah, but we've had a year to practice."

"And so has everyone else. There are thirty-one bands performing this year. I will just be happy if we are not last. So, let's aim for thirty."

"Or the top three," Megan replied.

"Megan, I love your optimism, and I really want to share it, but I can't right now. At least we are in the big city. We have what?" She looked at her watch. "Four hours until practice? We should get some hot chocolates and take a walk by the river. Maybe there will be some hot Bismarck guys there?"

"There's plenty of guys around here," Megan said, looking around the busy streets."

"Yeah, but it's all small town, bang guys. I've been there and done that, and it's so boring! Come on, it'll be fun! You can get whipped cream on your hot chocolate, my treat!"

"I thought you were not supposed to wander off," Megan said. "Isn't your mom worried about you being in the big city? That's why she came with you, right?

"She can be very overprotective at times. I'm not supposed to go anywhere *by myself*, and I'm not. You will be with me the entire time. Come on, I just need some air to breathe. How am I supposed to play the trumpet if I don't have air to breathe, Megan?"

She loved her mother but wished she could have some space. She was allowed out of the hotel without her mother following her around, but she still couldn't do what she wanted. She was sure her mother had other people out there keeping an eye on her, too—other adults.

"You make no sense, and I don't want to find a Bismarck boy, but you had me at hot chocolate."

The young woman smiled and held her elbow out. The two girls walked arm in arm down toward the river. Bismarck was busy with the band competition. Bismarck had three school bands entered into the competition, and another twenty-eight had joined from the surrounding area. The outside was filled with teenagers having fun, and most of the buildings were filled with music as each band practiced before the big event.

"There," the young woman said, spotting a small converted shipping container. A window had been cut out the front to serve hot drinks. "Two hot chocolates, please, one with extra whipped cream."

"Um, creepy guy to our left," Megan said.

The young woman looked over to see an older man standing amid the trees, looking over at both of them.

"Is that what you meant about finding a hot Bismarck guy?" Megan asked.

The young woman giggled. "No! Come on, let's get out of here before he comes and talks to us."

"We need to be careful, you know?" Megan said. "I've heard there can be some real creeps out here."

"I can handle myself. My dad put me in self-defense classes when I was three years old. Besides, look at him."

Megan glanced over her shoulder.

"He's not in the best shape," the young woman continued. "If he gets too close, we chuck our hot chocolates at him and run. No way is he catching the two of us."

"I'll be fine," Megan noted. "I was two seconds faster than you in the 800 meters."

"Any chance to slip that into the conversation!" The young woman looked over her shoulder to see the large man slowly walking after them. She wasn't scared, but she would keep an eye on him. It was relatively busy, so he wouldn't attack them, but maybe he had eyes on her purse.

The young woman sipped on her hot chocolate and walked at a brisk pace, just in case. They took the path down by the frozen river, and that reminded her of home. She was only away for a few days, so she didn't miss it. She knew, eventually, she would leave the town, and while she did want to get out, she was sure she would miss it then. They passed through two rows of bushes, and the path split.

"Come on," the young woman said.

And now, I can only think that my mother was right about everything. Why can't I be right about everything?

The two started running, turning toward the river on the next path and taking the path lined with trees for some cover.

"Is he still following us?" Megan asked.

"He might not have been following us at all," the young woman noted. She looked back over her shoulder but could not see anyone.

"I know, but it's better to be safe than sorry." Megan looked behind, too. "Good, he's gone."

The two women turned around and gasped. The young woman pulled her hand back as she thrust it in the air, and hot chocolate flew up from her cup, but it didn't land on the man in front of them.

"Sorry!" the young woman gasped quickly. "Someone was following us, and we thought you had caught us. I mean him. We thought he had caught us. I'm sorry."

"No need to worry, the man said. Here, give me that." He took the cup of hot chocolate from Megan and handed her a handkerchief in its place. You spilled some on your pants." He looked at the young woman and smiled. "You, on the other hand, have wonderful reactions. I thought I was going to be covered in hot chocolate, but your reaction is lightning quick."

"Self-defense classes," the young woman replied. "See, Megan, useful for more than just self-defense."

Megan smiled mockingly back up at her friend as she bent down to wipe as much hot chocolate from her white snow pants as she could.

"Cute dog," the young woman said. "Is he friendly?"

"She," the man corrected. "And, yes, she is a big teddy bear. Would you like to pet her?"

"I don't know if I should."

"Don't worry, it's fine. Here, give her one of these, and she will be your best friend forever." The man reached into his pocket and pulled out a small bone-shaped treat, handing it to the young woman.

"Maybe we should go," Megan said.

The young woman didn't want to go—the longer she could stay from the center of town, the longer she could stay away from her mother's watchful gaze.

"In a second," the young woman replied. "Are you a good girl? Would you like a treat?" She held her palm out flat, and the large dog licked it up from her hand. "See, Megan! Besides, that creep will not come after us with this dog around." She patted its head gently before scratching under her chin.

"Can we go?" Megan asked.

"Yes," the young woman moaned. "Come on, let's go."

"Oh, don't forget your hot chocolate," the man said, handing it back to Megan.

"Yeah, thanks," she replied.

The two women hurried off together.

"Is it just me, or is everyone in Bismarck creepy?" Megan asked.

"At least I didn't cover him in hot chocolate," the young woman laughed. "I got the fright of my life."

"You owe me another hot chocolate after this one," Megan said. "I wouldn't have spilled so much if you hadn't screamed so loud."

"What! You screamed first!"

"I did not!" Megan took a drink and pouted. "I spilled all of the whipped cream. That's the best part."

"Don't worry, I'll get you an extra large one next time with extra whipped cream on the top."

"I like the sound of that."

"Megan, are you okay?"

She looked around, her heart beating faster. She wasn't prepared for anything like this and suddenly felt like a young girl again in search of an adult, and not an eighteen-year-old who was supposed to be an adult.

"I don't feel so good," Megan said. She dropped her cup and fell to the ground, bracing herself on all fours in the snow.

The young woman looked around, and the man with the dog was right in front of her again.

"What happened?" he demanded.

The young woman tried to breathe. "I don't know. She looked pale and then just collapsed."

"Go to my car. Do you see the blue one in the parking lot?" The man pointed. "There's a first aid kit in there. Go and grab it and bring it back to me; the car is unlocked."

"Okay," the young woman said. She took off running toward the car. It was calming to be acting instead of panicking.

"Here, get her up onto that bench," the man said to someone else from behind her.

The young woman reached the car and pulled on the handle, but the door didn't open. She spun around, and the dog was before her, snarling ferociously. The young woman tried to cower back, but the car was behind her.

What is going on?

She couldn't see Megan anymore; the man was blocking her view.

"What are—?" she muttered.

He grabbed her, putting his hand over her mouth, as the car clicked unlocked and opened the door before shoving her in. The dog followed, hopping up onto the back seat and snarling at the young woman. She didn't dare move in case it bit her.

Mom, I need you! please!

The man got into the front seat and started the car.

"What did you do to her?" the young woman stuttered.

"She will be fine," the man said as he pulled out of the park. "Take off your shoes."

"What?" the young woman asked.

"Take off your shoes," the man demanded. When there was silence, he added, "Control!"

The dog inched forward and barked at the young woman. Saliva dripped from its teeth and muzzle—the young woman could not look away. And it did not look like only saliva dripping from the dog's muzzle; there was a pinkish hue to it.

"Control!" the man snapped as he drove.

The dog inched forward again until it was almost touching the young woman. She could feel the warmth of its breath, and there was a look of evil in its eyes.

The young woman was frozen to the spot, but she knew she had to act. She didn't want to find out what happened if she didn't comply.

I don't want to die!

She reached down as slowly as possible, not breaking eye contact with the beast. She untied her shoes and handed them forward to the man. He took them and tossed them on the front seat.

"Release!"

The dog stopped growling and sat back a little, still watching the young woman. She was terrified for her life. The man had poisoned Megan, and now he was taking the young woman somewhere. The young woman looked out the window as they drove but didn't dare make a sound. No one knew she was gone yet, and even when they did, they would not know where she had been taken.

"What do you want with me?" the young woman asked.

"I need to take your happiness," the man replied.

CHAPTER NINETEEN

Kelsey was woken from staring out the window and daydreaming as they drove in search of the orphanage's former owner. She took her phone from her pocket and answered it.

"Hello?"

"You left me a message to call you back, and it sounded urgent," the woman said.

"What's your name?" Kelsey asked.

"Linda Donaldson."

"You were in Brookside Orphanage at some point, right?"

"Yes, I was. What is going on? Am I in trouble?"

"No, you are in no trouble, Linda. Can you tell me where you are right now?"

"I live in Miami."

"Okay, that's good, Linda. Do you have any family there?"

"Yes, my husband is with me right now," Linda replied.

"Do you have any children?"

"I have one daughter, but she moved out a year ago."

"And where is she now?"

"Is she in trouble?" Linda asked.

"No, no one is in any trouble. I need to ask you a few quick questions, and then I am going to give you a number to call. You will speak to Officer Marcy in the Vanburgh County Sheriff's Office, and she will explain it all to you. There has been some trouble in our area, but you are so far away that you don't need to worry about it, okay?"

"Okay," Linda replied, a little more at ease.

"Does your daughter live close?" Kelsey asked.

"No, maybe an hour away."

Kelsey smiled. "Good, you must see her reasonably often." If she was an hour away from her mother, she was also safe. For now.

"I do; we spend every Sunday together."

"Linda, have you been contacted recently by anyone who was at the orphanage?"

"Um, no. I don't see anyone from there, and I moved to get away from it. The only person who contacted me was Trevor about five years ago."

"Trevor Goldson?"

"Yes, he wanted to speak about the lawsuit, but I was done with that part of my life. I wished him well. Maybe if I lived in the area still, we could have gotten together and talked about it more. Maybe that could have helped."

"Helped?" I asked.

"I was so sad to hear about his death. Maybe I could have helped. I was at the orphanage with him for a couple of years. I didn't remember until he called me. He was a sweet kid, and I liked him. He was a few years younger than me."

"Did Terrance Knox ever call you after Trevor did, Linda?"

"No, but he was at the orphanage too. I remember him. He was pretty broken. Of all the kids, he was punished the most. He would do all he could to get into trouble; he didn't like people telling him what to do."

That sounded like Terrance.

"Were they friends?" Kelsey asked. "Trevor and Terrance?"

"Yeah, they were pretty good friends, from what I remember. They both came five or six years after I got there. I'm glad they had each other."

"Is there anything else you remember about your time there?" Kelsey asked. "From what I have heard, things were not easy."

"I don't like to think about that anymore. I try to think of the good times as much as I can. When I first arrived, I had a copy of Oliver Twist. By Charles Dickens?"

"I know the book. A story of an orphan, right?"

"Yeah. I loved that book. Of course, it was taken from me when I got to the orphanage, but I used to recount the story to the younger kids—I had it memorized almost word for word. They renamed me after him! Isn't that a hoot?"

"I'm glad you remember it fondly," Kelsey said. "Let me give you the number I want to call."

When she was done with the call, Kelsey sighed.

"Good or bad?" John asked.

"Mostly good," Kelsey replied. "She's far enough away that she's in no immediate danger and has done her best to be happy with her life. That must be the fiftieth person I have spoken to. To be honest, I wish more people had moved away—resources are being stretched thin if we allocate officers to each former resident with a family. There are only so many families we can keep an eye on."

"So, we catch the scumbag before he strikes again," John reminded.

"We do," Kelsey replied.

We try!

"You ready to go in?" John asked.

Kelsey nodded.

Pine Meadows Care Facility sat atop a hill above the town of Jonesville, just outside Vanburgh County. It was a care facility for seniors who needed round-the-clock care. It was also where Brian Finnegan, the former owner of the orphanage, resided.

They checked in at the reception desk before being shown to one of the main living areas where a dozen old people were spread out. There was a smell in the place, a smell of death. Old people moved around on walkers; one had an intravenous tube connected to her arm, and another pulled around a large oxygen canister. It was a place where people came to die.

The orderly pointed over to a large gentleman in a wheelchair. "That's him."

"Thank you," Kelsey said. She had the utmost respect for people who helped others like this, even if some were scumbags.

"I guess he's not the killer unless he's faking it."

"No, he's not the killer," Kelsey said.

They went over to the window where Brian sat looking out.

"Brian Finnegan?" Kelsey asked.

"Yeah, who wants to know?"

"I'm Special Agent Hawk," Kelsey said, showing her badge. "And this is Deputy Sheriff Gallant. We would like to ask you a few questions."

"About what?"

"About Brookside Orphanage," Kelsey replied, sitting down on one of the cushioned chairs by the window.

"Yeah? What about it?"

"You used to run the place, didn't you?" Kelsey asked.

"Yeah, ran it until it closed."

"Liked to hurt the kids there, didn't you?" John asked. "You and your dog."

"Tough love," Brian smirked. "Different times back then. You couldn't do that now. No wonder kids are growing up like they are. In my day, people were strong. Doesn't matter. It's all gone now."

"We could arrest and try you for what you did to those kids," John said.

"You could try. They tried that one, and it didn't go anywhere. I didn't do anything wrong."

"Making them go out into the cold, having your dog chase them, punishing them for wetting the bed. How many children did you abuse in that place?" John demanded.

"Kids nowadays have it far too easy."

"So, you don't deny it?" John asked.

"You can talk to my lawyer if you want to ask questions like that," Brian spat back.

He might have lost the use of his legs, but his mind was still sharp.

"Why did you burn it down?" Kelsey asked.

Both Brian and John looked surprised. Kelsey was surprised she had put it together, but it felt right.

"Was it because of the guilt or because you wanted to hide what you did there?" Kelsey continued.

"You don't have proof of that," Brian said quietly.

"You don't deny it," Kelsey said. "Start answering our questions, or I will reopen the investigation into the arson. Are you going to be more cooperative?"

Brian looked at Kelsey, back at John, and then out the window. "I've answered all of your questions, haven't I? They won't put an old guy like me in prison now."

"You liked it, though, didn't you? Torturing the kids. We both know you will get away with it, but admit for once in your life that you enjoyed it."

Brian turned back to Kelsey with a dark look in his eye. "Oh, I loved it. I wish I could have done more, but they took it from me."

"Investigated and closed you down."

"Yeah," Brian admitted. "Then someone, not me, burned it down a few months later. It was probably an insurance job."

"What happened to the dog?" Kelsey asked.

"They wanted to put it down, but I saved her. Best dog there ever was—that thing could smell fear."

"It can't be still alive," Kelsey noted.

103

"Nah, it died years ago but lived a *very* full life before then. They used to whisper that it devoured children. I wish it did. Made the best guard dogs."

"You bred it," Kelsey said.

"You're a quick one," Brian replied. "Made a good living off that dog and her offspring after they closed down the orphanage. There's still a little bit of her out there in the world. In fact, had a guy come in and buy one of her grand-pups a while back; he claimed he was in the orphanage. So, it can't be all that bad, eh? You want them to hate my guts, but they are better for it."

"Who bought one of your dogs?" Kelsey asked. She took a picture of Terrance Knox from her bag. "Was it this guy?"

"I don't know, could have been."

"When did he buy the dog?" Kelsey pushed.

"Must have been about three years ago, right before my family stuck me in here. I tried to raise them well, but I didn't have the same methods at my disposal. They take your kids away from you now for that sort of thing. Then they turn around and stick me in this place— wouldn't have happened if they had been raised right."

He wasn't helpful, but the last piece of information was. She believed the owner's reign of terror over the children ended when the orphanage had, but he was loosely connected. Another dog was out there, and she was confident it had ended up in the hands of the killer.

"We won't get anything else useful out of him," Kelsey said. She stood up and walked out, John following after her.

"We visit Terrance again? Or his property? See if one of the dogs is there?" John asked when they were outside.

"I don't know. There are a couple of things bugging me."

"Why would someone from the orphanage go to his tormentor and buy one of the dogs?" John asked.

"Everyone deals with trauma in their own way. I think the killer bought one of the dogs, and they are using it to terrorize young women or young women *so far*. He grew up without parents, and the staff at the orphanage were all he had. He would have been abused, threatened, and hurt, but he respected it in his own twisted way. Maybe he was punished more than the rest, and he wants to terrorize the others. No, it's something else. Maybe he can't move on with his life after what happened. But he sees everyone else moving on. It hurts him more than the orphanage. He wants them to be traumatized like he is. That's why he doesn't kill the former residents. He doesn't want them dead; he wants them to suffer, and he wants to make their families suffer in the same way he suffered."

"How do people get this messed up?" John asked. "I believe what you are saying, but I really hope you are wrong about it."

The name Linda Carlson had given her continued to run through her head, nagging her to make sense of it. There was more there than just a nickname—a connection that told her what might be coming next.

"Oliver Twist," Kelsey muttered. "Oh, no, no, no!"

"What is it?"

She was named after the character, but she was a girl, not a boy.

"They named her after Oliver Twist, but they would have called her Olive Twist."

"Who?" John asked.

"Linda Donaldson. She would have been Linda Carlson back then, but they would have known her as Olive Carlson in the orphanage. They named her after Oliver Twist, and if the killer was in the orphanage with her, he might know her by that name and not her real name. If he is searching for children who went to the orphanage, he would have found a match for Olive Carlson and not known to look for Linda Carlson."

"Liv Anderson used to be Liv Carlson," John commented.

"Exactly. Olive Carlson. Where's the Sheriff's daughter right now?"

"Bismarck," John replied. "She's there for a band competition, but Liv is with her."

"I want you to call the Sheriff and go straight there—Sheriff Anderson's daughter might be in danger."

"What are you talking about? He's targeting people from the orphanage. Neither of her parents are orphans."

"No, but he thinks they are. Liv is with her, right?"

"Yeah."

"Maybe she is safe. They would be around the same age, and when he looked her up, he would have looked up Olive Carlson instead of Linda Carlson."

"Her maiden name," John murmured, putting it together too. "Liv Carlson, short for Olive. He wouldn't take her! The Sheriff's daughter?"

"I don't know," Kelsey replied. He's targeting people in the area. She might be next on his list. Go there now and bring Liv and her daughter back to Winchburgh. I want you to be there for the Sheriff

105

too. He is already stressed and under pressure, but when he finds out about this, he will need someone."

"Where are you going?" John asked.

"I need to talk with Terrance again. He knows something, and I intend to find out what it is. If he knows something about the killer, I will get it out of him."

"So, he's not the killer?"

"I wish he was. He's cuffed to a hospital bed—that would make our lives very easy. Go as quickly as you can. Get on the phone with Liv, too, and call me as soon as you know they are safe."

"Be careful," John said.

"I always am."

John gave her the same smile he had given back at the hospital. Kelsey was lying. She was careful when needed, pushing past that when it meant catching the bad guy. Her previous SAC, Paul Granger, was still on her back, watching her every move from afar and waiting for her to mess up.

If the county sheriff's daughter was taken, or worse, murdered, it would be the perfect fodder to get her kicked out of the FBI for good.

Kelsey would do everything it took to ensure that didn't happen.

Everything.

CHAPTER TWENTY

"You need to come with me," Kelsey said. "I'm giving you one chance to escape."

Terrance looked up at Kelsey from the bed with disbelief in his eyes.

"What sort of trick is this? What game are you playing?"

"No trick, no games, Terrance. I know you haven't done anything wrong. I would have acted the same if you had come to my residence with guns drawn. If you had killed me or the deputy sheriff, you would have been well within your rights with private property laws. Why do you think I aimed for your shoulder and not your chest?"

"What private property laws?" Terrance asked.

"We don't have time for this," Kelsey hissed. "Deputy Gallant is on his way down here now to question you again, and he ordered me to stay at the station. Is that what you want? Do you want to be alone in a room with him?"

"I… what are you going to do? We can't go out the window."

Kelsey smiled. "We are going to go out the front door. Walk straight on out. I forged some transfer papers and gave them to the cops outside. When the deputy gets down here, he'll know they are fake or fight them if he thinks they are real. Either way, he'll keep you here. This is a one-time-only offer, Terrance. Either come with me now or stay here."

Terrance still hesitated.

"Fine, have it your way." Kelsey turned and walked for the door.

"No, wait!" Terrance called after her. "Okay, okay. What do we need to do."

"You need to be quick and do exactly as I tell you, Terrance." She took the key from his pocket and removed the cuffs from his hand and the hospital bed. She handed him the bag of the clothes she had brought. "Put these on quickly. If John gets here before we get out, it's my ass on the line. You go to prison, and I probably do too. We escape together, okay?"

"Alright," Terrance said, a look of hesitation still in his eyes.

Kelsey turned around so Terrance could get dressed, and he moaned a little as he put the shirt on. He would be in pain for some time still. At least she had the jump on him. If he tried anything, she could subdue him with his injured shoulder. Kelsey turned back around to find him fully dressed.

"Put these back on." Kelsey tossed him the handcuffs.

"What? Why? What are you going to do to me?"

"I'm going to free you," Kelsey hissed. "How would it look if I transferred a prisoner through the hospital without his hands cuffed? If I wanted to kill you, I would have done it while you were still cuffed to the bed. The cops at the door saw me in here with you, and I'm caught on camera, so there is little point in springing you from this place only to kill you. They would know it was me."

"Maybe you are going to make my body disappear."

"For what, Terrance? We are running out of time here. You didn't hurt anyone, did you? Unless you want to confess to any crimes? Either put the cuffs on, or I cuff you back to the bed, and you talk with the deputy. I don't think he will have as sympathetic an ear."

Terrance calculated in his head, and he begrudgingly put the cuffs on. Kelsey pulled him toward her with the chain between the two metal loops and secured them as tight as they would go.

"Good, now walk out with me and don't say a word, alright?"

Terrance nodded.

Kelsey led him between the two officers.

"Goodnight, boys. Go home to your wives," Kelsey said to them.

They both nodded at her and smiled. The document one of them held was perhaps the only truthful thing she had said to Terrance. When Kelsey told Terrance that she had faked his transfer papers, she meant it. She couldn't work with the local law enforcement or the hospital staff in Jamestown. There was no chance they would let her take Terrance out on a little field trip. The transfer papers were a lie, as was everything else she had told Terrance.

Kelsey tried to keep as calm as possible as they walked out. John wasn't coming—he was on his way to Bismarck—but if someone else questioned her, her story might not hold up. All she had to do was get out of the hospital and drive away from it so she could do whatever it took to make the next part of the plan work.

The air was cold and biting when she got outside, as it had been every single day since she had arrived in North Dakota. She held Terrance's arm and led him to her car. She opened the passenger door and made a show of holding his head so he wouldn't bump it as she helped him in. She didn't want to put him in the back—this was her car, not a cop car, and there was no metal mesh between the front and back. She didn't need Terrance thinking something was up and grabbing her from behind as she drove. Kelsey got in on the driver's side.

"Can we take these off now?" Terrance asked.

"Soon," Kelsey replied. "I don't want anyone to see me put you in my car and then uncut you." She started the car and drove out of the hospital parking lot.

So far, so good.

"We need to make a stop at my house," Terrance said. "I have some stuff to pick up before we leave the state. Which direction do you want to go?"

"I don't know yet," Kelsey admitted.

"I could see it in your eyes when you came to my place. You don't trust them either, do you?"

"I don't trust anyone," Kelsey admitted. That was not true. She had not trusted anyone back in Valleyview and didn't trust anyone when she arrived in Winchburgh, but she trusted some people now. The sheriff and the deputy, anyway. She prayed the call would come soon and his daughter was safe.

"My family was killed," Kelsey continued, needing to keep him from getting suspicious. It felt more natural to tell the truth rather than make something up. "My parents were murdered, so I guess you can call me an orphan, too. My sister was killed. They didn't find who killed them."

"See, that's just what I tell everyone. They're off clinging to their power instead of finding the criminals. I lost half my life to that orphanage, and they didn't do anything about it. They should have chucked them all in jail, but they didn't. He's still out there somewhere, and I hope he's rotting in hell."

"We visited him in a nursing home," Kelsey said. She didn't know why she was telling him this. Because she was an orphan, too? Because she wanted him to let his guard down? Because she could see how much pain he was in? He might be a criminal who had hurt people, but only because he had been hurt. If he helped her find him, would that redeem him?

"Who?" Terrance asked when Kelsey had been too quiet for too long.

"Brian Finnegan, the former owner of Brookside Orphanage. He's in a wheelchair now. He's in constant pain, too," she lied. "Doesn't remember who he is most of the time, but he is on constant bedrest and takes painkillers night and day. They had to put his dog down years ago. He wets the bed too and has to have someone come and clean it."

"Oh, that is too funny!" Terrance shouted. He burst out laughing and was genuinely happy for a brief moment. "Good! Good!" Terrance rocked back and forth in his seat. "He deserves it. He deserves to live the rest of his life in pain. I've thought about it for so long. I wanted to find him and kill him—I dreamed about it—but this is far better. He got what he deserved, and they will all get the same."

"Where is he?" Kelsey asked.

"Who?" Terrance replied, turning serious again.

"You know who I am talking about, Terrance. You know he is killing them, and you know it is wrong. I knew you would never tell us while stuck in the hospital bed with two cops for protection, but I hope you will tell me now that it is just the two of us. Come on, I told you about Brian Finnegan—you can tell me where he is, and all of this will be over."

"I… I don't know what you are talking about," Terrance said.

"Yes, you do, Terrance."

"You can just leave me at home, and I can go the rest of the way alone." Terrance looked out of the window. "We're not going to my house, are we?"

"I'm taking you to the Chester Bridge."

"Why?" Terrance asked nervously.

"I was hoping the beautiful view might help you think a little clearer."

"Maybe I will talk to Deputy Gallant," Terrance asked.

"No," Kelsey said. "He's on his way to Bismarck right now. It's just you and me, Terrance."

"What are you going to do?"

"Whatever it takes," Kelsey replied.

Terrance moved quickly to grab the wheel, but Kelsey slammed him back into the chair with her arm. Terrance winced in pain and bent his head toward his wounded shoulder. Kelsey slammed her arm into him a second time to remind him who was in charge. Terrance groaned but made no move to try and do anything stupid a second time.

"I don't know anything," Terrance cried out.

Kelsey remained silent and continued to drive. Terrance let out a groan from time to time as she shifted in his seat, trying to get comfortable. Kelsey could almost hear him trying to work out how he was going to get out of this. Her phone rang, but she didn't pick it up.

"I don't drive all that well in the snow. Don't want to answer and go off the road," she warned.

Twenty minutes later, they made it to Chester Bridge. Kelsey parked on a small secondary road facing the bridge.

"Move an inch, and you will get a lot worse than last time," Kelsey warned.

If he wanted to get out, he would have to unbuckle his seatbelt first and open the door, all with a damaged shoulder. Kelsey grabbed her phone and played the voicemail from Deputy Gallant.

It's not good. You were right, Hawk. Liv just called, and her daughter has been taken. They don't know what happened yet but are talking to her friend Megan. Megan was drugged in a park by the river—we don't know about Felicity. They were speaking to a man with a dog, and they think he took Felicity. Megan gave us a description of the man and the dog. I don't know; it could be Terrance. I'm on my way to Bismarck now, Sheriff Anderson too. He's taken pretty much the entire town to look for her. Get here as quickly as you can. I'll call you if we find her. He took off in a blue car; that's all we know.

Kelsey felt her blood boil. She blamed herself for putting it together too late. She couldn't—there was nothing she could have done.

"It's gone beyond the killings," Kelsey said. "He messed up this time. He's taken the Sheriff's daughter. She's innocent in all of this. Neither of her parents was at the orphanage. I will give you exactly twenty seconds to tell me what I want to know; that's about how long it should take to get to the edge, right?"

"What?" Terrance gasped.

Kelsey didn't wait. She slammed her foot on the gas and took off toward the small cliff that dropped into the ice river below.

"Say whatever prayers you need to because I am not stopping until you tell me where he is!" Kelsey cried as they hurtled toward the edge.

Terrance gripped onto the seat and moaned as his shoulder hurt again.

"Ten seconds!" Kelsey called when they were almost halfway to the edge.

"Alright, I know where he is!"

"I can't hear you!" Kelsey shouted.

"I know where he is!"
"Who?"
"Trevor Goldson!"

CHAPTER TWENTY ONE

Kelsey slammed on the brakes, and the car skidded toward the edge until they could no longer see the ground in front of them. The car rocked to a halt but didn't tip. Kelsey kept the engine running. Terrance breathed heavily, still grabbing the seats and staring straight ahead.

Kelsey had to grip the wheel tight as she reeled from the shock. It was one thing to threaten to drive over a cliff under the assumption of a hunch and another to have it confirmed. They were killed by a ghost, but a living, breathing ghost.

"Tell me where he is hiding out," Kelsey demanded.

"I don't know," Terrance said. "No, wait, wait! I don't know for sure, but I *might* know where he is. Just give me a chance."

Kelsey's emotions flipped back and forth from shock to outrage. He had faked his own death to be free to kill others. It sent a shiver racing up her spine.

"Make it quick," Kelsey said.

"He came to me about a year a—"

"Quicker!" Kelsey demanded, slamming her fists on the wheel. "Or we both end up drowning in a river as he supposedly did."

"Okay, okay," Terrance gasped. "I told him about some unoccupied places in the area. He will have gone to the house in Beckor Woods; it's got power and everything. He'll be comfortable there for as long as needed.

"No, where else?" Kelsey asked. "Somewhere off the grid. No light, no heat, just like at the orphanage."

"There are a couple of places like mine that are fenced off, so you can't get a vehicle down to them."

"No, not them. He has a vehicle. Off the grid, and where a car can get to. Where is that?"

"I guess he could go the old Wilkins cottage, but it's in rough shape."

"Like the orphanage?" Kelsey asked.

"Yeah, I guess."

"Take me there," Kelsey said.

"Okay, start by backing up from this cliff, please," Terrance said, still terrified. "Get back on the highway and head south."

Kelsey did as she was told, carefully ensuring the car was in reverse before she pressed on the gas. She spun around and slammed on the gas once she was facing in the direction they needed to go, not caring about the speed limit. The conditions were not great, but Kelsey was willing to risk her life to get there in time. Risk both their lives.

Kelsey took her phone and sent Deputy Gallant a message, even though looking down at her phone put them in more danger on the icy roads.

"What's the name he is using?" Kelsey asked. "He must have changed his name, right?"

"Kenneth Smith," Terrance muttered, still afraid of Kelsey's driving.

Kelsey returned to her phone again and called the Sheriff's office.

"Marcy," she said when it was answered.

"What do ya need, hun?"

"I need you to look into someone for me. This is a top priority, okay? His name is Kenneth Smith. If you can find it, I want to know everything for the past year: credit cards, bank statements, properties, vehicles, and phone records. There might be a few people with the same name, but this is an individual who created a fake identity, so look for anything suspicious. Now, before you do that, see if you can find his phone and track where he is. I need to know if I'm going in the right direction."

"You got it, hun. I'll call you as soon as I get a ping."

"Thank you, Marcy," Kelsey said.

"I didn't think it was him," Terrance uttered.

"But you suspected it, didn't you?" Kelsey noted. "You are an accessory to murder, Terrance."

"I'm cooperating with you."

"Only after I threatened to kill you, Terrance. If it turns out we are going to the wrong place, well…."

There was dead silence in the vehicle. Kelsey knew she wouldn't kill him if they went to the wrong place, but she would ensure he was punished to the full extent of the law.

"How did you know about it?" Terrance asked.

"I could see it in your eyes," Kelsey replied. "It was the way you spoke. You are such a frickin' idiot, do you know that. You can't go around distrusting everyone."

Even if it is what I have done for so long.

"It was what you said, too," Kelsey continued. You said you knew something we didn't. You didn't say things; you said things. You had one piece of information we didn't. Deputy Gallant thought you were talking about the government and all that nonsense, but it was about Trevor. You mentioned a ghost. You couldn't help yourself, could you? I put two and two together. I looked into his file, and there was never any body found. He faked his death so he could cause misery for those who were at the orphanage, didn't he? Did you help him with the death?"

"No, I was shocked when I heard about it. We spoke a lot on the phone about the lawsuit, and then, one day, I got a call telling me he was dead. We had a memorial and everything. When he showed up on my doorstep last year, I thought he was a ghost. I was scared out of my mind, but he told me he needed a place to crash. I let him stay at my house for a night, but he wouldn't stay longer. He was uncomfortable all the time in his own skin. He told me he had another way of making things right, but I didn't think it would be this. Even when I heard about the death of Becky Samson, I didn't think it was him. Even now, I can't believe it is him behind this. He told me not to tell anyone about him being alive, or I would be punished too. It wasn't just him; he had this dog with him. I wanted to speak sense into him, but...."

"It was like being back at the orphanage again, wasn't it?"

"I thought it was the same dog. I was terrified. It had the same evil look in its eye, the same bloodthirst. He made it pin me to the wall just to show me what it could do. He wasn't the same man I once knew. I should have called someone. Maybe, I don't know. I was scared of him. I still am. I was scared of the dog. If I had—"

Kelsey's phone interrupted the conversation. She picked it up.

"Marcy, what do you have for me?"

"I found a phone that could be his. It was registered under the same name, but it's been switched off for a while. The last ping puts it at the gas station on Leven Road."

"The gas station on Leven Road?" Kelsey asked Terrance.

"That's close to where we are going," Terrance confirmed.

"Okay, Marcy, keep looking, alright? That's a great help, but the more you find out about him, the better. Is anyone else there right now?"

"It's just me, hun," Marcy said. "With the terrible news from Bismarck and officers out checking on those other families, we are stretched pretty thin."

"Alright, call me if you find anything else."

"You got it, hun."

Kelsey was on her own for now. She patted the holster in her jacket—the gun was still there. She might have to take down a man and a dog. She couldn't shoot a dog the last time, but she knew she would kill this one. It was as evil as its master. History was repeating.

"I thought he might try and scare them into joining the lawsuit," Terrance uttered. "That was all I thought. I thought it was just a coincidence with the death."

"Well, you thought wrong," Kelsey said.

"Did he really kill Cecily Brown too?" Terrance asked.

"I believe he did. I think he led her away from the barn dance and used his dog to strike fear into her. He herded her like a sheep, keeping her in the field with no shoes or jacket until she froze to death."

"That's what they tried to do to us in the orphanage," Terrance muttered.

They were the same but from different worlds. Kelsey was orphaned when she was ten, but she had been taken in by an aunt. Would she be a completely different person if she had been sent to an orphanage instead? Would Terrance? How about Trevor Goldson? If he had family who would take him in, would he be doing what he was doing? Would he be as messed up?

"There's the gas station," Terrance said.

Kelsey stared at it as they passed, hoping to see a blue car, but there was not one. Tim was never on their side, but it might be this time. Trevor was bolder in how he took her compared to the others. Maybe he was washing her and saw how careful the sheriff and his wife were being. He had to wait until she was more alone.

He would need somewhere secluded to take her and do what he wanted to do. This was not the end of his work—he had lots more people to terrorize. He didn't know they knew he was still out there, and that gave them some time if he was taking her from Bismarck to his hideaway; that gave them even more time.

But it was the Sheriff's daughter, and he must know that even if he didn't realize he had taken the wrong person. He would know there would be people after him.

Kelsey didn't know what it all meant but hoped he wouldn't see them coming.

"Turn just up here," Terrance said.

There were no markings or road to drive down, only a space between some trees. When Kelsey turned onto it, the snow was compacted and flat. If he were down this road, he would feel safe. He would believe no one would find him unless Terrance gave him up, and even then, he might think Terrance didn't know where he was for sure.

"Stop here," Terrace said. "See the bend up there? He'll be able to see us from the house as soon as we are around it. We'll need to go the rest of the way by foot."

"*We?*" Kelsey questioned. "You are going nowhere near this."

"You don't have any backup, do you?"

"I don't care. I don't care what information you gave me; I still don't trust you. You've helped, but you're still his friend. You still share a bond with him. No, you are staying here."

"You don't trust me enough to come in with you, but you trust me enough to leave me in the car?" Terrance asked.

"No, I don't trust you enough for that," Kelsey admitted. She pulled out her gun and pointed it at him. "Get out."

"What are you doing?" he asked.

"Get out!" Kelsey ordered.

Terrance unbuckled himself and got out of the car. Kelsey did the same, keeping the gun pointed at him as much as she could. She took the keys from her pocket and tossed them to him.

"Unlock one side," she ordered. "And don't worry, I'm a pretty good shot, but you know that. I shot to wound last time; I will shoot to kill this time."

Terrance held her eye but did as he was told.

"Hands around the tree," Kelsey said.

Terrance hesitated, but he did as he was told. He hugged the tree, the cuffs dangling from one wrist. His arms fit around the young tree and no more.

"You know what to do," Kelsey said.

Terrance grimaced. He replaced the cuff on his free wrist so he was tethered to the tree. When he was bound, Kelsey went to him and took the keys back.

"I wouldn't have run off," Terrance claimed.

"Now, you definitely won't," Kelsey argued.

"So, you are going in there alone?"

Kelsey checked her gun, loading a couple more bullets into it.

"What if you don't come back?" Terrance asked. "What if he kills you, and then he comes for me? I'm a sitting duck out here. At least leave me a weapon."

"You don't get any sympathy," Kelsey said. "You might not have killed anyone, but you let this happen. You better hope that I am as good as I know I am. I will protect you as much as possible, Terrance, but I can't let you go. Not just yet. If he's in there, you will have some redemption, but you could have stopped this."

Kelsey turned and started through the snow before Terrance could say anything. She had the same feeling as when approaching Terrance's house, but there was one main difference. The man in this residence, if he was in fact there, was far more dangerous.

CHAPTER TWENTY TWO

Kelsey pointed her gun at the house, scanning it for movement. She hoped the Sheriff's daughter was still alive; this would completely tear the town apart if she were not. They needed Sheriff Anderson, but he would no longer be the same person. The death of her family had torn Kelsey apart; it would do the same to the Sheriff, and once he was torn apart, Winchburgh would be torn apart.

The fear filled Kelsey's stomach. It was multiplied exponentially. She had been sacred at Terrance's house when she thought he might be the killer, but she was much more afraid here—she was sure Trevor Goldson was the killer. She was afraid because this was not just another victim, not just a local woman, but the Sheriff's daughter. She was most afraid that she would be too late. She might take the killer down, but another death could haunt her.

She saw nothing. No movement in the windows, no sign of a dog. Complete silence all around except for the tapping of a woodpecker somewhere in the forest. She held her position in the trees, hoping to see something to better know which side to approach from. Kelsey circled around to the right, his heart pounding furiously in her chest. She moved until she was facing one corner of the house, the angle giving her the best chance of not being seen from any windows.

Kelsey was about to step forward when her instincts told her to look down. The laces of her boot were touching a thin metal wire. She moved her foot back and stepped over it. When she was on the other side of the wire, she traced it to the bottom of a tree trunk attached to a hand grenade—the perfect warning and maiming system. Kelsey unhooked the hook from the grenade pin in case someone else followed her.

This won't be the only trap out here. Death might be around every corner.

Kelsey checked the windows once more, but there was nothing. However, it was hard to tell with the glare bouncing off them, reflecting the trees and rich, blue sky. The adrenaline pumped through her veins, and she did not feel the cold. Trevor Goldson did not feel the cold either, but he welcomed it—Kelsey might be able to get inside his head, but she did not welcome the cold.

There was no time to stand and think; if she was going to act, she had to do it quickly. The more she hesitated, the more time he had to kill her. He had taken his time before and planned it out, but that did not mean he would do the same this time. Kelsey took one final breath to steady herself and pushed the fear deep down into the pit of her stomach. She scanned the ground in front once and then took off sprinting.

She expected the crack of a rifle, but there was none. Either he had not seen her coming, or he was waiting inside for her to come in.

Or he's not even here, and Terrance has led me to the middle of nowhere so Trevor can complete his task.

Kelsey stood with her back to the concrete wall, and the cold permeated through her jacket, causing her to shiver. She sidled along it, ducking down when she got to one of the windows at the front of the house. She peeked into it, just as she had done at Arnold Sanchez's house, and found the same thing: nothing. No, it was less than nothing. No jacket hung over a chair or a dirty plate on the dining room table. The house was dark inside, and it did not look lived in. The dining room was attached to the kitchen, and there was no one in there either. An open doorway led to a short hallway on the other side of the dining room, and Kelsey kept watch for a moment, hoping to see a small shadow or movement. When she saw nothing, she continued down the front of the house.

There was no glass or peephole in the front door. Kelsey ignored it for now and continued along the front of the house. She moved to the second window on the front and peeked into that one as carefully as the first. She found a bedroom, also unlived in. The bed had a mattress but no bedcovers or pillows. Another open door led to another small hallway that must have connected to the first. An open door partially must have led to a bathroom.

Still, there were no signs of life—no shadows or movement.

Kelsey only had one option: the front door. She slid back along the wall until she was to the side of the door with the hinges. She reached out and took the knob, turning it gently. When it was turned enough, the door clicked open. Kelsey quickly removed her hand and gripped her gun, pointing it toward the small crack. If he had booby-trapped the woods, there was a good chance he had booby-trapped the front door, too.

Kelsey saw the wire near the corner of the door. Perhaps he was at the back of the house and did not know she was there. Perhaps he had booby-trapped the house and left, or someone else had. She had not seen a car, but it might be around the back or parked in the trees somewhere to keep it out of sight.

There was no time to disable the trap. She might be able to reach around and follow the wire with her fingers, but it would take too long, and she would have to put her body close to what was behind the door. Her best guess was some sort of gun rigged up to fire. He would not have another grenade, not for an entrance he also used.

Please let me be right!

Kelsey stood with her back to the wall to the side of the door and kicked her foot back to open the door while dodging to the side. The gunshot was so loud that she thought someone had fired right by her ear. The shotgun splintered the wood, sending the door flying closed. She needed the element of surprise. Kelsey kept low in case there was another shot and barged her shoulder into the broken door. She rolled into the dining room, coming back up with her gun pointed deeper into the house.

Steady breaths, steady breaths!

Kelsey listened, the gunshot still ringing in her ears. If they were here, they would have heard that. She remained crouched, ready to take him down, but no one appeared. No sound of someone escaping through the backdoor, no barking of a dog, no struggle of a young woman who knows rescue is here. Nothing!

Kelsey stood up quietly. It felt colder inside the house. Everything fit with the killer, but he was not there. No one was in the house. It was not just the cold or silence; it was the feel of the place. Kelsey was sure it was empty. She let herself relax a little but didn't lower the gun.

The dining room was the largest room in the house. The table filled most of it, and there was a fireplace on the outer wall with a pile of firewood beside it, but no blackened burnt lots were in the fireplace. A map of the area hung on the wall beside a painting of silver birch trees standing among the snow.

Kelsey poked her head into the kitchen, but it was empty. She worked her way through the house, clearing the rooms one by one until she was in the bedroom. Kelsey crouched down to look under the bed, but no monsters were there. That only left the closet. She opened it and stepped to the side, expecting someone to jump out at her, but it was empty, too, except for a threadbare blanket.

She picked it up and smelled it. She moved to the switch on the wall and flicked it, but no light came on. If Trevor Goldson wanted to recreate his living conditions from the orphanage, this was the place to do it.

The clatter from the kitchen startled her, and he pointed the gun immediately at the door.

You don't get away!

Kelsey sprinted through the house. If he were waiting for her in the kitchen, he would have a clear shot at her, but she would have time to get off a shot, too. She bounded into the kitchen, her heart pumping, and came face to face with a squirrel. It chirped in fright and scampered out the open window. Kelsey saw the spoon on the floor that the rodent had knocked down.

She looked out the window as the squirrel escaped, its prints lost in the snow. The sun glared off the white, a blanket of purity that cleaned up the world. Everything was lost and hidden out there. She tapped the spoon against the wooden countertop.

He has to be here. If he is not here, then...

Kelsey didn't want to think about it, but if he was not at the house, he was killing her somewhere else.

She sniffed the spoon, and in an instant, she regained hope. She opened the cupboard doors, finding one empty cupboard after another, until... cans of dog food—a dozen or so of them. She grabbed one and checked the best-before date—good until next year.

You are close, aren't you?

Kelsey dropped the spoon and ran outside the back of the house to check if they had made an escape in that direction. She had not seen anyone leave out the front. Either they had gone into the wilderness, or she was too late, and Trevor had driven out onto the highway before she got to the house.

The tracks were not visible from the window but led away from the house. They were faint, slowly being covered by the wind. He had been here with his dog and had ventured out into the wilderness with Felicity. Kelsey drew her phone from her pocket and pulled up her map app, but it wouldn't load. She saw the lack of signal on the top bar: no data or service. She was all alone out there.

But so is Felicity!

Kelsey ran back inside and into the dining room. She tore the map down from the wall and spread it on the table. Using the roads they had driven on, she was able to find the approximate location of the house. And not far from it was a river.

The river where he will take her to kill her.

She knew only the approximate direction, but it was the best she would get. Kelsey ran back through the kitchen and out the back door. She followed the tracks for as long as possible and then ran toward where she hoped the river was.

Before   it   was   too   late.

CHAPTER TWENTY THREE

Trevor Goldson gripped Felicity around the neck as he revved the skidoo to take it to the river. He wore little clothing, and neither did she, and with her back pressed to his front, the warmth of her body transferred to his—it brought life and could save them if they did not have a way out of the white wilderness. Trevor despised the heat. They had a way out: Trevor would go back the way they had come, and Felicity would not.

He had to act quickly. She was the Sheriff's daughter, and they would all be out looking for him. They did not have the first clue who he was or where he was hiding, but someone might stumble upon the proverbial needle in a haystack. He would dispose of the girl and the house and move on to somewhere else. His work was almost done in this area—those who needed to be punished had been punished.

They did not deserve a life so happy. They did not deserve to live normal lives when they had also been abused and beaten as children. Who were they to live as if nothing had happened? Did they not know how to understand and show their pain?

Life was pain, cold, dark. Only death would set them free. He licked his icy lips as he remembered the grief embedded on the faces of the Browns. How delicious it had been to be deemed an accidental death. It gave him some breathing space to enjoy their pain and plan for the next one, but time was not on his side anymore.

Still, the Browns displayed their pain, the pain life brings. The Samsons, too. The Andersons would finally understand what life was supposed to be like.

Warmth in front of him and warmth behind. He could feel the heat radiating from the beast sitting in the large cargo basket. It was man's only faithful companion, but even the beast did not understand pain. It knew rage and death, but it did not have anything to be stripped away. No family, emotion, or dignity. It was nature's perfect animal—incapable of pain and suffering. Humankind would be much better off if they were all reduced to animals.

Trevor switched hands, placing his right hand on Felicity's neck and his left on the other side of the handlebars. The cold was biting into his exposed flesh, and he might lose another finger this winter. Felicity gasped through the fabric stuffed in her mouth as the hands were switched.

He could feel her shivering against him. It gave him no pleasure. She did not need to be shown what life was—the young woman was an unfortunate pawn in a much bigger game. If her mother lived like she was supposed to, a wounded and broken animal, her daughter would not be in this position. People wore masks, hiding who they truly were. It was the only way to unmask her.

Trevor let the skidoo naturally slow down, and when they were almost at a stop, he squeezed on the brake. The vehicle came to a stop with a slight shake. He looked around. It was completely white in every direction, the sun glaring off the snow. The sky was bright and blue, but there was no warmth in the day. It was perfect.

Trevor got off the snowmobile first. Two beasts were still on it, and both were docile and cooperative. They would both revert to their animalistic side soon, but only one would be controlled with a command after that. Another reason why beasts held the upper hand. They had primitive intelligence.

"Control!" Trevor ordered.

The large dog changed in an instant. Its nostrils flared, and teeth were bared. It turned its head, remaining in the warmth of the basket, and growled at Felicity. Her torso jerked when she heard the growl, but she did not dare look behind.

Trevor walked a few paces from the skidoo and dropped to his knees in the snow. He bowed forward until his forehead touched the cold. He scooped up snow in both hands and dropped it onto his head to bathe in the chill. He took two more handfuls and rubbed the snow over his head, working it into his icy, brittle hair. The warmth of the ride was stripped away, and he felt more like himself again.

He remained in the same position for a few minutes, his forehead pressed to the snow. Every so often, he scooped more snow over his head. He was finally ready. He stood back up, shaking his head to remove most of the snow. He went back to the vehicle and took Felicity by the arm, pulling her from her seat. She flinched and moaned through her gag when her bare feet touched the snow.

"You will get used to it," Trevor asserted.

Felicity closed her eyes tightly and started to sob—her body jerked back and forth as the tears rolled down her cheeks. Trevor leaned forward, watching as the small streams froze to the woman's cheeks. It was the most beautiful sight in the vast landscape. He let her cry some more—the emotion should have been her mother's, but the daughter was showing it instead.

When her body stopped jerking back and forth with the sobs, Trevor untied the rope around her wrists. She was good, just like the others, and did not move. The gun in the holster around his waist scared her, but not as much as the snarling beast still sitting on the skidoo. Bullets had a chance of missing, but the dog never missed.

He left Felicity for a moment and went to the dog. He placed a hand on its head. The beast never once looked away from its prey, a red glow in its eyes. Slobber fell from its gums and jaws, sticking to the plastic-covered metal basket and freezing solid. Felicity still shivered, but the movements were not sobs anymore; the deep cold had taken root. Soon, the cold would take her in its icy grasp, and she would not notice it anymore.

"It's time," he said to Felicity.

He went to her and removed the gag. She had seen where they had come from and where they had gone—there was no use in crying out. No one would hear them, and no help was coming.

"Please," Felicity stuttered. "Please, I'm so cold. M-my shoes."

Trevor nodded in understanding. He could see the change in her as she understood the pain.

He looked down at her bare feet, pale with a tinge of blue.

"It will not last long," he assured. "The cold is already taking the pain away. Your mother and I both suffered like this when we were younger, but she has hidden it away. She does not remember what they did to her."

"I don't understand," Felicity sobbed. There were no tears this time.

"You will," Trevor replied. "At the end of your life, you will have understanding."

"Please don't kill me," Felicity begged.

"*I* will not kill you. The cold will claim you, but this is because of your mother. You have to die so she can truly live. Your sacrifice will release her, my dear."

Felicity's eyes flicked to the dog and back.

"Your guide." Trevor smiled. "The beast is evil, just like the devil-spawn that chased us, but the path it leads you down is good. Do not look into its eyes. Do not look back when it chases you—it will only make things worse. Only look forward, okay?"

He could see the look in her eyes; she did not believe this was for the best, but he knew it was. He felt it all coming back to him; could hear them shouting at him; could feel the strike of a hand across his cheek; taste the bile in his throat as he tried to get the food down. He looked her up and down one last time—she was dressed in rags and scraps with no shoes, just like they had been when they were far younger. Trevor wore little clothes out in the snow, and he did not feel the cold anymore. He wore shoes, but only for grip—he did not want anything to go wrong; her death should be as pleasant as possible.

"Go," he whispered.

Felicity's eyes opened a little wider.

"Go!" he screamed.

She closed her eyes tight before she turned and ran down the bank of the river. Trevor ran after her.

"Come!"

The command brought the dog to his side. Felicity was fast—she was an athlete too, a privilege afforded to her that he and her mother had not been gifted. It was good. The farther she ran, the more he could run with her and relive his memories.

He could almost feel the warm breath of the beast on the back of his neck from when he was a child. It's spawn ran with him now. It wanted to kill her, to tear the flesh from her bones, but he would not let it. Would it devour the woman if given the chance? He did not know, but it was not a part of the plan.

"Herd!" Trevor called. "To the river!"

The dog quickened its pace, moving around to the side and front of the woman. It barked viciously, and Felicity tripped and fell into the snow. She was back on her feet instantly and ran down the shallow bank to the ice-covered river. Trevor hoped she did not plunge through into it. That had slowed down the last victim. He wanted the best of both worlds. Cecily had been held in place by the dog until she had succumbed to the cold, but there had not been space to make her run. Becky had run, but she had plunged her foot through into the water, quickening the process. The ice was thicker here, so it should hold. She would run until she could run no longer, run into the open arms of the cold, and die a slow, numb death.

He would grieve for her first, and then enjoy the family's grief.

He could not wait for the frozen death mask to cover her face and the glassy eyes to look back at him from the world beyond.

CHAPTER TWENTY FOUR

Kelsey's legs burned. It felt like she was running through deep water—the snow was a foot deep. It had been hard going at first, but lifting her leg now took all her effort. The deep snow dragged her down with each step, and the cold worked up her body. She could no longer feel her toes, and even though she wore thick gloves, she had also lost sensation in her fingers. She could not stop to warm herself or put her hands in her pockets as she ran—she had to keep going as fast as she could.

This was one time when it really was a matter of life and death.

She might have felt the fear if Kelsey could feel anything except the cold. There were two beasts out there: one animal spawned from an animal of evil and another who channeled evil. She had not been able to take out Terrance's dog, but she would not hesitate with this one. And then there was Trevor Goldson, the man who had felt cold and pain in the orphanage as a child, just like the others. From how he had killed the other women, he wanted them to feel the cold, and she was sure he embraced the cold as his ally. Kelsey already felt her dexterity sapping away. Would she have enough left in her to take down both beasts?

Her breaths were so shallow that they were barely visible in the barren landscape. The white had been beautiful before, but it felt like death now. It welcomed her with open warms just like Cecily and Becky, just like it was about to welcome Felicity.

The thought drove Kelsey on. She had lost her strength long ago and had no idea how long she had been running. She had no idea how far it was to go. She held the FBI trainee record for the half marathon, conducted on grass and in the sun while wearing running shoes. It felt like she had covered a marathon already, even though it was likely less than two or three miles.

The scream that came from her left was the most welcome sound Kelsey had ever heard. It meant that Felicity was in danger, but it also meant she was still alive. Kelsey stopped and turned to her left, running toward the scream, and her legs ached more—screaming out that they couldn't keep running.

Much like Kelsey ignored the orders of others, she ignored the complaining of her legs. The pain distracted her from the cold, and the cold distracted her from the pain. The snow got deeper where it had been blown against the small ridge, and Kelsey slowed to a quick walk. It was more painful—she had to push through the snow instead of stepping through it, too deep to lift her leg out.

It felt futile when she got to the top of the small ridge. They looked so far away. Even though she could not identify them, she knew it was Felicity being chased by a large dog with Trevor Goldson just behind. Kelsey pointed her gun down toward them. Felicity was sluggish, her whole body sore from running and whatever abuse she had suffered previously. The dog was not sluggish. It kept a slow pace behind Felicity, barking and occasionally nipping at the back of her feet, but it didn't properly bite her. Trevor Goldson called out to the dog, but Kelsey could not make out the commands.

She pointed the gun at Trevor, but he was too far away. There was no guarantee to hit him, and with the distance and wind, she could easily hit Felicity by mistake. It didn't matter how sore and tired she was; she had to get closer.

Kelsey trudged through the snow again, pushing as hard as she could. The blue sky and bright sunshine did little to lift her mood, and the sun seemed to burn cold in the sky. Kelsey made it to the top of the ridge and pushed through the last of the snow before she lost balance and rolled down the small bank. Her back hit the firmer ground—the frozen river. She grabbed her gun and stood up, her body aching all over. Her legs complained some more when she took off running again, and while it was constant agony, it felt like she was floating. There was only a covering of an inch or two on the ice.

She was behind them, and she would not be seen unless Trevor turned around. The wind whipped up now she was out in the open. She was numb, but the wind still cut and bit at her cheeks. Even from a distance, she could see how little Felicity and Trevor were wearing. It was not just about saving her from Trevor but from the cold, too.

Kelsey looked behind and was sure she saw a head just above the ridge before it ducked down behind. She didn't see his face, but the only conclusion was Terrace had got free and was after her. He would not have ducked down if he were there to help her. He didn't have a weapon, but he might still pose a problem. He didn't matter for now,

130

and if she continued to run, he would not catch her before she stopped Trevor.

She was going to stop Trevor. She had to!

Kelsey was closer—Trevor was only moving as fast as Felicity—and she raised her gun again. She might hit him from that distance, but there was still a chance she would hit Felicity, who was directly in line with Trevor.

The ice beneath her foot released a sharp crack but did not break.

Suddenly, Trever spun around with a gun in hand and fired at her.

Kelsey dived to the side, rolling in the snow as bullets whooshed past her. She somersaulted to one knee, breathing out as she fired back. Her aim was way off, the shaking in her arm making her shots unpredictable. She ducked down again when the gun was pointed, and bullets peppered the ice around her. Kelsey heard a crack and lurching noise. She pushed herself back to her feet as the ice cracked beneath her and stumbled forward onto more solid ground.

The dog was still chasing Felicity, but Trevor had become a little separated. Kelsey fired again but missed as Trevor took off after his prey. He now knew she was behind him and would try to kill Felicity as quickly as possible before he made an escape. If he kept running, he would escape—Kelsey couldn't keep running like this for much longer.

Only one chance to catch him.

Kelsey sprinted with the last of her energy and chased them down. She ducked her head to the right as she was fired upon again. Trevor swung back and forth between trying to shoot her and catching up with the dog.

Kelsey had two choices: stop and try to make the shot or run faster to catch them. If she stopped and took down Trevor, she would be too far away to stop the dog from doing anything. She could not fire while running at top speed, especially with the shake in her arms.

Trevor stopped and spun around again, taking more careful aim this time, and fired. Kelsey felt her arm jerk to the side as the bullet connected, but she felt no pain—most of her body was numb. She saw red on her jacket but had no idea how bad the wound was. She kept running as Trevor deftly took another clip from his pocket and exchanged it with the spent one, even though he was not wearing any gloves.

"Kill!" Trevor commanded.

Kelsey felt a numb shiver run up her spine when she thought he was sending the dog after her, but the command was not to kill the *pursuer* but the *pursued*. She was close enough to take a better shot, even with the tremors in her body, but Trevor was not the main threat anymore.

He reloaded to shoot at her again, but the dog was going for the kill.

"No!" Kelsey screamed. She fired toward the dog, unloading her full clip, and without any feeling in her fingers, she managed to reload quicker than Trevor could and fire toward the dog again, cutting through the ice a couple dozen times.

"No!" Trevor screamed.

His attention was taken, and he looked away from Kelsey, searching for his companion. She fired near the dog again, and it yelped in fright. It was hesitant and moved a step tentatively closer, but when she fired to the left of its leg, it whined and sprinted through the deep snow in the opposite direction.

Kelsey pointed her gun at Trevor, only a few feet away, but there was only a click when she pulled the trigger. He swung his gun up, and she threw hers. He raised his hand to deflect it, and it was enough to get close. She picked up the speed as much as her legs would take her and leaped through the air. When she slammed into him, it felt like she had thrown her body into a block of ice. She lifted him off his feet, and they flew through the air, smashing into the bullet-ridden ice and plunging straight through it.

Hitting Trevor had knocked the wind from her, but hitting the water almost knocked the life from her. She had not only hit the water, but it felt like the icy death had come up to hit her back.

The water below was not deep, but the momentum and the rushing current of the water below spun them around and took them under the ice. The cold ripped her body apart—it felt like shards of ice impaling her when she was submerged. Tiny slivers of light cut their way through the water from the clear patches of ice above, but the darkness swallowed them quickly.

Kelsey banged on the ice, trying to punch her way through it, but it was impossible. She tried to recall anything that would help her, searching for a point of light, but everything was murky and dim. She scrabbled around, hoping to find the opening by accident.

She saw it—a ray of light. And she saw him swimming toward it. Kelsey spun around and swam against the current. If she was sore, she didn't notice. Everything felt like a dream, like she was not in her own body anymore and was swimming through thick syrup. It was warm, too. She reached out and grabbed his foot. He kicked at her, but she did not let go and kicked as hard as she could to pull him back from the hole. She was staying down there and going to keep him down there, too.

He yanked his leg from her grip, and suddenly she was face-to-face with him. He smiled at her before reaching out with both hands and clamping them around her neck. The rumbling above felt like thunder.

Kelsey was too numb to feel herself being choked. She reached through the gap between his wrists with both arms to lever his hands from her neck. Before he could grab her again, she grabbed the collar of his t-shirt and pulled him toward her, spinning herself quickly to be behind him. She wrapped her legs around his waist and one arm around his neck, creating a t-bar hold. Kelsey could feel the current taking her farther and farther from the opening.

There would not be time to return to the opening; there would only be time to ensure he did not kill anyone else. Her heart panicked, beating a hundred times faster than normal, but her mind did not. In a moment of clarity, she didn't understand how she could accept her death so readily. Perhaps the cold had numbed her completely. Still, her body was fighting not to shut down.

She was not angry at her oncoming death—there was peace as long as he succumbed too. His death would make it all worth it.

He wriggled in her arms, jerking around like a large fish on the end of a hook. Kelsey found strength she did not know she had. She held him tight, and he could not break the grip, no matter what he did. She took his strength—as he weakened under her hold, she held him tighter and tighter.

Even when the life was drained from him, she held him for ten seconds more just to be sure. Then, she released him into the current and pushed him from her. Salvation was gone, the opening was too far, and the strength she had been gifted was only enough to stop Trevor Goldson's reign of terror. The ice was clear enough above her to float under the surface and see the blue sky above. She would bang on the ice if she had any strength left, but she knew there was no getting through it.

Zip! Zip! Zip!

Kelsey saw the bullets fly by her head in slow motion. They whizzed through the ice and slowed before falling gently toward the river bed. Five, six, seven, and then too many to count. Nothing for a moment, and then more bullets came through the ice. A final gap and two dozen more bullets. There was another boom like thunder, and the world became noisy again.

A hand grabbed Kelsey's and pulled her from the ice. The cold hit her, then the sunlight. She blinked and looked up into the eye of her savior: It was her sister, but she was grown now and alive somehow. No, not her; she only came in Kelsey's dreams.

She blinked. It was Terrance.

Kelsey was helped out of the water and onto the ice, and everything hurt again. Kelsey tried to stand up, but he was unable, and she stumbled forward onto her hands and knees. She was on the other side of the ice this time, and she didn't see blue. She saw eyes. The lifeless eyes of Trevor Goldson buried beneath the ice. The beast was removed from the world.

"Felicity?" Kelsey whispered.

Before she could get a response, the white turned to black.

CHAPTER TWENTY FIVE

Kelsey moved in and out of consciousness. There was white all around, and she was still numb, but she was slightly warmer. There was a noise, a dim hum as if the world was shaking—the skidoo traveling with her on it. She couldn't move, not even her eyes. She tried to find the source of the warmth and noise but could only see a blur of white snow as it rushed past her.

White, then black. And black then white. Alternating like a chessboard. She was the queen, and the king and knight were gone— she had captured them.

She screamed herself awake—she was back in the small house she had explored. The monochrome was gone, a raging fire in its place, consuming everything before it. Still, she could not move. The scream came again, but it was not from Kelsey.

Kelsey was in enough pain that she might have screamed in agony if she had not encountered such pain. This time, it was physical—in the past, it had been physical, mental, and emotional. She was used to pain. The fire before her was created to warm her, and her body slowly returned to temperature. She remembered it all: running through the snow, tackling Trevor and his dog, killing Trevor.

"It hurts so much!" The woman beside her wailed her words and sobbed between them.

Kelsey thought she was dreaming. She had enough warmth in her body to turn her head. Felicity was beside her, both of them in damp underclothes. They each had a threadbare blanket wrapped around their shoulders. Felicity had her knees up to her chest and was rubbing her purple feet—it would be agony as they defrosted. Kelsey started to cry, too.

"Thank you," she whispered, overjoyed that Felicity was with her now. "Thank you, thank you, thank you."

More warmth and energy flooded back to Kelsey, and she shuffled over to close the distance between them and put her arm around Felicity. The warmth doubled.

"It will be painful, but you will be fine," Kelsey whispered, her teeth chattering.

"He was going to kill me. He would have killed me if you had not come. He wanted to make me like Becky, didn't he? I was so scared."

"You don't need to be sacred anymore," Kelsey said. "You are safe now." She held Becky tight. "I thought I'd lost you. How did—?"

The creak of the door stopped Kelsey mid-sentence. Her body jerked, but she was powerless to do anything else. She didn't relax fully when she saw Terrance.

"I thought I heard sirens," Terrance said. "Help is coming to us."

"How did you…? Why did—?" Kelsey chattered.

"Help you?" Terrance finished. He walked to the fire with an oven glove and took hold of the pot balanced on a metal grate. He removed the pot of boiling water and took it behind the two women to the dining table. "Deep down, I knew what he was doing, but I didn't let myself believe it. I couldn't. When you cuffed me to the tree, I thought about those women and how he took them and kept them captive, and something about that made it seem more real. And I just… wanted to make sure you were okay. You could have killed me when you took a shot at me, but you chose not to. I figured I owed you one, even if I did give you the information you wanted. Sometimes, you have to trust people."

"Yeah, I'm learning that too," Kelsey admitted.

"Here, take these, but drink them slowly, alright? They're very hot," Terrance said, passing Kelsey and Felicity steaming hot mugs of tea. "One of the advantages of living off the land is knowing how to start a good fire and which leaves and pine needles are best for making tea. It doesn't taste like Orange Pekoe, but it'll warm you both up."

"How did you escape?" Kelsey asked.

"I have my ways." Terrance winked. "Like I said, knowing how to survive in the wilderness has advantages."

Kelsey knew he wouldn't tell her, and she tried not to show her frustration. She was sure she would work it out in time.

"I thought you were dead," Terrance admitted. "Dragged you out of the water, and you looked like death itself. Needed a ghost to kill the ghost. Found the dog on the way back, too—damn near ran itself to death—thought it was dead when I saw it lying in the snow. I almost took my hand off when I tried to pet it, but when I went back to the skidoo, it hopped in the back before I could get on. I thought the whole way home it was going to go for my neck. I had the three of you in the

136

vehicle with me, and I prayed the entire way back that at least one of you was alive."

"Where's the dog?" Kelsey asked.

"It went into the house when we got here and had enough energy to hop up on the bedroom bed before it flowed down and fell asleep. I closed the door to keep it in there. I don't want to be the one to wake it up. I don't know what comes next for that beast."

"We'll do our best to rehabilitate it. It was only obeying its master—we'll see how it reacts with a more tender master," Kelsey said."

"You saved my life," Kelsey said.

"You saved her life," Terrance said, nodding at Felicity. "And who knows how many others."

"Why did he choose me?" Felicity murmured.

"Sheer bad luck," Kelsey replied. "He thought your mother was someone else. You shouldn't have been in any danger, but he thought your mom went to the orphanage he did. It was the worst possible mixup that could have ever happened." Kelsey sipped some of the tea, and it felt like molten lava dripping into her stomach. "Did he hurt you, Felicity?"

"He kept me tied up; that's all. He took my shoes and some of my clothing. He told me he wanted me to feel the cold. Megan! He poisoned her! I think he killed her!"

"Don't worry, Megan is fine. He wanted to get to you."

Felicity let out a trembling breath.

Kelsey held her even tighter.

The sound of sirens came from the distance, and for the first time in days, Kelsey felt like everything was going to be fine. The killer was dead, and the killing would stop. The town would have to deal with the death of Becky Samson and the fact that Cecily Samson had also been killed, but the Sheriff's daughter had been saved.

Red and blue lights lit up the interior of the small, desolate house. The door burst open a moment later, and Sheriff Anderson entered the room.

"Daddy!" Felicity burst into tears.

"Oh, my dear," Sheriff Anderson cried. He went to his daughter and lifted her to her feet, wrapping the blanket around her and embracing her tightly.

Kelsey couldn't help crying, too. She found enough strength at the sight before her to rise to her feet. She checked her arm; the pain was starting to come back now that she was warming up. The bullet had taken some of her flesh, but it was only a deep graze—she would heal quickly from the injury.

"I thought I had lost you," Sheriff Anderson said. "I went to Bismarck to look for you, and you were out here, helpless. I'm sorry, my dear. I'm so sorry."

"I thought I was going to die, Daddy! He was going to kill me. He was going to kill me!" Felicity started to cry and hyperventilate at the same time.

The sheriff rubbed his daughter's back until the medics entered to tend to Felicity. Kelsey pulled the blanket around her, finally finding warmth from it. She felt a whole lot of emotions running through her. She had saved Sheriff Anderson's daughter and had been saved by Marcy. She was relieved to have made it in time and was thankful to Marcy, but the overwhelming emotion was the sheriff's love for his daughter. And from the way he looked at Kelsey, he had love for her, too.

The Sheriff took Kelsey in his arms and held her tight, just as he had done with Felicity.

"Thank you," the Sherif whispered.

Kelsey could not reply; she was overcome by emotion. It was not the love from the sheriff but the thought that he had become like a father in her life in the short time they had known each other.

"Sorry," he said when he let her go. "I shouldn't have just grabbed you like that."

"No, it's fine," Kelsey replied. "It's good. I need a little more of *this stuff* in my life to balance the other stuff."

"My daughter would have died if it wasn't for you," Sheriff Anderson said. "I will never be able to thank you enough for that, so know that I am eternally grateful. That doesn't mean you can come to work late now and take longer lunch breaks. I know I'm not technically your boss, but I will still be a hard ass as sheriff."

Kelsey laughed, and it hurt her muscles. "You are a good man," she said.

She reported to the SAC in Bismarck but thought of Sheriff Anderson as her boss. The SAC in Bismarck pretty much left her alone to do her job, while Sheriff Anderson played a big part in how she worked. Both were far better than her former SAC in Valleyview, the man who was still out to get her. Saving the sheriff's daughter and stopping another serial killer would keep him off her back for a while.

Kelsey melted a little more when Deputy Gallant entered. It was stupid to react like that, but she was glad to see him again later, coming close to death. She was getting closer to many people in town but was closest to him.

He strode over to her and wrapped his arms around her, and she immediately became aware that she was in her underwear beneath a thin blanket. Hugging the sheriff had been like hugging her father, but hugging John was different. It was more intimate. He was married, but she knew it was not a happy marriage. She would never do anything to jeopardize his relationship, but if…

She did not let herself think it. She had almost died but was still alive, and she should bask in that for a while.

It's going to take a lot more than that to kill me.

She and John didn't say a word as they embraced. She leaned her head on his shoulder, and the warmth came seeping back.

EPILOGUE

Being trapped under a thick sheet of ice in rushing water was torture, but it meant the regular cold of Winchburgh, North Dakota, did not seem as terrible as it had when Kelsey had arrived. She was not used to it yet but could live with the snow. Still, she hoped she never had to run through it ever again.

She took a deep breath and pulled the blankets tight around her neck to trap all the warmth. Felicity was safe and would fully recover, just as Kelsey would. They were both on bed rest for the next five days, and then they would be checked over again. Kelsey had always been driven to work as hard and as much as possible, but she liked the idea of finally taking a rest.

As long as the town was quiet. She would be out of bed in a flash and back to work if there was a hint of trouble. For now, she could happily deal with watching bad TV movies and eating junk food. Her body and mind needed a break. The Sheriff had invited her over for supper once she had recovered fully. He and his family were still coming to terms with the fact Felicity had been targeted because of a mix-up.

There would be vigils for Cecily and Becky once the town had some time to breathe, and there was still Terrance Knox to sort out. He faced jail time for endangering two law officers but had been instrumental in stopping Trevor Goldson. These were all things Kelsey was thinking about but not things she had to deal with yet.

Her phone rang, and she picked it up from the table beside her bed.
Caller Unknown
Kelsey didn't know why, but it felt ominous. She hit the answer button.

"Hello?" Kelsey said.

"Special Agent Hawk?"

Kelsey recognized the voice on the other end of the line: Harvey Waters.

"Mr. Waters," she replied. "Have you changed your number so I won't call you anymore?"

"The other line was not safe," he said.

The tone of his voice told her something was wrong or had happened.

"I'm listening," Kelsey said.

"There's much more to your problem than you know," Harvey said quietly. "Much more to it that I know. I can't talk about it over the phone, but there are some details that you don't know."

"My family?"

"Not on the phone," Harvey warned. "I don't know what's going on, but someone is covering up something. I can't say anymore here. Can you meet me?"

"Where?" Kelsey asked. "When? Yes, I can meet you."

"I'll come to you. Don't mention this to anyone, and you don't say my name to anyone, okay? If you do, you won't hear from me ever again. Do I make myself clear?"

"Crystal," Kelsey replied.

"I am on my way to North Dakota now. I will be in touch very soon, Special Agent Hawk."

The line went dead. Kelsey stared at the screen, but he was gone.

Kelsey felt scared.

Apprehensive, scared, anxious, but a little hopeful.

NOW AVAILABLE!

DEAD TO ME
(A Kelsey Hawk FBI Suspense Thriller—Book Three)

Tough and brilliant FBI special agent 30-year-old Kelsey Hawk is relocated to the desolate and unforgiving land and endless highways, hitchhikers are turning up dead—and Kelsey may be the last hope to save the next one in time....
scape of small town North Dakota, to which she'd vowed to never return, when, along the remote
"This is an excellent book... When you start reading, be sure you don't have to wake up early!"
—Reader review for The Killing Game

DEAD TO ME is book #3 in a new series by #1 bestselling mystery and suspense author Kate Bold, whose bestseller NOT ME (a free download) has received over 1,500 five star ratings and reviews.

When she was just a child, Kelsey's entire family was murdered, leaving her, the sole survivor, to grow up in the foster system. A rising star in the FBI, Kelsey set her ambitions on being assigned to a field office in the big city, away from the ghosts of her past. But when she's reassigned to a small town in North Dakota, she can't help but remember all the tragedy she fought so hard to leave behind.

Can she stop this killer in time?

A page-turning and harrowing crime thriller featuring a brilliant and tortured FBI agent, the KELSEY HAWK series is a riveting mystery, packed with non-stop action, suspense, twists and turns, revelations, and driven by a breakneck pace that will keep you flipping pages late into the night. Fans of Rachel Caine, Teresa Driscoll, and Robert Dugoni are sure to fall in love.

Future books in the series are now available.

"This book moved very fast and every page was exciting. Plenty of dialogue, you absolutely love the characters, and you were rooting for the good guy throughout the whole story... I look forward to reading the next in the series."
—Reader review for The Killing Game

"Kate did an amazing job on this book and I was hooked from the first chapter!"
—Reader review for The Killing Game

"I really enjoyed this book. The characters were authentic, and I see the bad guys as something we hear about daily on the news... Looking forward to book 2."
—Reader review for The Killing Game

"This was a really good book. The main characters were real, flawed and human. The story went along quickly and wasn't mired in too many unnecessary details. I really enjoyed it."
—Reader review for The Killing Game

"Alexa Chase is headstrong, impatient, but most of all brave with a capital B. She never, repeat never, backs down until the bad guys are put where they belong. Clearly five stars!"
—Reader review for The Killing Game

"Captivating and riveting serial murder with a twist of the macabre... Very well done."
—Reader review for The Killing Game

"WOW what a great read! Talk about a diabolical killer! Really enjoyed this book. Looking forward to reading others by this author as well."
—Reader review for The Killing Game

"Page turner for sure. Great characters and relationships. I got into the middle of this story and couldn't put it down. Looking forward to more from Kate Bold."
—Reader review for The Killing Game

"Hard to put down. It has an excellent plot and has the right amount of suspense. I really enjoyed this book."
—Reader review for The Killing Game

"Extremely well written, and well worth buying and reading. I can't wait to read book two!"
—Reader review for The Killing Game

Kate Bold

Bestselling author Kate Bold is author of the ALEXA CHASE SUSPENSE THRILLER series, comprising six books (and counting); the ASHLEY HOPE SUSPENSE THRILLER series, comprising six books (and counting); the CAMILLE GRACE FBI SUSPENSE THRILLER series, comprising eight books (and counting); the HARLEY COLE FBI SUSPENSE THRILLER series, comprising eleven books (and counting); the KAYLIE BROOKS PSYCHOLOGICAL SUSPENSE THRILLER series, comprising five books (and counting); the EVE HOPE FBI SUSPENSE THRILLER series, comprising seven books (and counting); the DYLAN FIRST FBI SUSPENSE THRILLER series, comprising five books (and counting); the LAUREN LAMB FBI SUSPENSE THRILLER series, comprising five books (and counting); and the KELSEY HAWK MYSTERY series, comprising five books (and counting).

An avid reader and lifelong fan of the mystery and thriller genres, Kate loves to hear from you, so please feel free to visit www.kateboldauthor.com to learn more and stay in touch.

BOOKS BY KATE BOLD

KELSEY HAWK MYSTERY
DEAD INSIDE (Book #1)
DEAD RECKONING (Book #2)
DEAD TO ME (Book #3)
DEAD SILENCE (Book #4)
DEAD TO DAWN (Book #5)

ALEXA CHASE SUSPENSE THRILLER
THE KILLING GAME (Book #1)
THE KILLING TIDE (Book #2)
THE KILLING HOUR (Book #3)
THE KILLING POINT (Book #4)
THE KILLING FOG (Book #5)
THE KILLING PLACE (Book #6)

ASHLEY HOPE SUSPENSE THRILLER
LET ME GO (Book #1)
LET ME OUT (Book #2)
LET ME LIVE (Book #3)
LET ME BREATHE (Book #4)
LET ME FORGET (Book #5)
LET ME ESCAPE (Book #6)

CAMILLE GRACE FBI SUSPENSE THRILLER
NOT ME (Book #1)
NOT NOW (Book #2)
NOT WELL (Book #3)
NOT HER (Book #4)
NOT NORMAL (Book #5)
NOT AGAIN (Book #6)
NOT SAFE (Book #7)
NOT TODAY (Book #8)

HARLEY COLE FBI SUSPENSE THRILLER
NOWHERE SAFE (Book #1)
NOWHERE LEFT (Book #2)
NOWHERE TO RUN (Book #3)
NOWHERE LIKE THIS (Book #4)
NOWHERE GIRL (Book #5)
NOWHERE TO HIDE (Book #6)
NOWHERE CERTAIN (Book #7)
NOWHERE PURE (Book #8)
NOWHERE SOUND (Book #9)
NOWHERE SANE (Book #10)
NOWHERE TRUE (Book #11)

KAYLIE BROOKS PYSCHOLOGICAL SUSPENSE THRILLER
LAST BREATH (Book #1)
LAST CHANCE (Book #2)
LAST WISH (Book #3)
LAST SHOT (Book #4)
LAST MISTAKE (Book #5)

EVE HOPE FBI SUSPENSE THRILLER
IN HIS BLOOD (Book #1)
IN HIS SIGHTS (Book #2)
IN HIS REACH (Book #3)
IN HIS MIND (Book #4)
IN HIS WAY (Book #5)
IN HIS THOUGHTS (Book #6)
IN HIS DREAMS (Book #7)

DYLAN FIRST FBI SUSPENSE THRILLER
OUT OF REACH (Book #1)
OUT OF TOUCH (Book #2)
OUT OF TIME (Book #3)
OUT OF BOUNDS (Book #4)
OUT OF LUCK (Book #5)

LAUREN LAMB FBI SUSPENSE THRILLER
SOMETHING KNOCKING (Book #1)
SOMETHING CALLING (Book #2)
SOMETHING WRONG (Book 3)

SOMETHING DARK (Book #4)
SOMETHING TO HIDE (Book #5)

Made in United States
Orlando, FL
13 January 2024

42445058R00085